GRIZZLE'S
ST ~~GRIZELDA'S~~
SCHOOL
FOR GIRLS,
GHOSTS AND
RUNAWAY GRANNIES

STRIPES PUBLISHING
An imprint of the Little Tiger Group
1 Coda Studios, 189 Munster Road,
London SW6 6AW

A paperback original
First published in Great Britain in 2017
Text copyright © Karen McCombie, 2017
Illustrations copyright © Becka Moor, 2017

ISBN: 978-1-84715-813-0

Printed and bound in the UK.

2 4 6 8 10 9 7 5 3 1

GRIZZLE'S ST ~~GRIZELDA'S~~ SCHOOL FOR GIRLS, GHOSTS AND RUNAWAY GRANNIES

KAREN McCOMBIE

Illustrated by BECKA MOOR

stripes

For Naina, the Pickled Pepper girl!
— KMcC

To Woodsend
— BM

Chapter 1
St Grizzle's New Guest (Gulp)

And unicorn onesies...

It's hard to take your head teacher seriously when she's wearing a unicorn onesie.

Especially when the horn on her head bounces up and down when she's making a point.

"...and *that's* why we all have to remember to be kind and thoughtful to one another!" says Lulu – the head – stomping her hoof.

Today's topic for assembly is "**KINDNESS**". All the school is here in the hall, in their PJs and slippers, sprawled on the floor with random pillows, soft-toy buddies and scruffy bed-head hair as they tuck into their breakfast. At St Grizzle's we always have pyjama assemblies first thing on a Monday, cos Lulu thinks it gives the week a nice, relaxed start. I haven't been here all that long, so I'm still wow-ing at the difference between this and assemblies at my *old* school.

There, we had to sit statue-still, listening to stern, grey-suited Mr Robinson drone on about **"APPLYING OURSELVES"** or **"WHY HOMEWORK MATTERS"** while we were all going quietly demented with pins and needles in our crossed legs.

From the squashy comfort of my polka-dot pillow, I sneak a peek at my new schoolmates – everyone's listening very politely to Lulu's speech, even the eight-year-olds of Newts Class, who are wriggling and squiggling just the *tiniest* bit.

The only noise is the occasional crunch and spoon-clunk from those pupils and teachers who haven't finished their breakfast yet, and a loud **"OW!"** from May-Belle, who's just been headbutted off her beanbag by a goat.

St Grizelda's School for Girls – St Grizzle's to us – really isn't what you might call normal.

My mum assumed it was, when she packed me off here for three months while she went to study penguins' bums in the Antarctic. (She's a zoologist doing a project on why they waddle – she's not just staring at bums for fun.)

Mum chose St Grizzle's because she thought it was all about sensible uniforms, serious lessons and jolly-hockey games.

Instead, it's more about pyjama assemblies, classes in tree-house building and four-legged school mascots that eat anything, whether it's a recognizable food or not. (Yesterday, Twinkle the goat ate Mademoiselle Fabienne the art teacher's left shoe and a tube of magenta poster paint.)

Before she dropped me off here, Mum *also*

assumed St Grizzle's was big and busy and packed with plenty of perky students. But a few months ago, Lulu changed the style of the school and that wasn't too popular with one or two of the parents. OK, about a *hundred* parents, who took their kids out faster than you can say, "Oh, please give it a chance..."

So now there are only twenty names on the St Grizzle's school register.

The biggest class is the Newts (all ten of them), then come the Otters (i.e. the scary, starey triplets), then the Conkers (Yas, Angel, May-Belle and Klara) and finally Fungi Class – the oldest in the school, which consists of me and twins Zed and Swan.

I was pretty wary of Swan to start with. OK, I'm still wary of her now, to be honest, even though she's totally cool and my friend and everything. She is super-smart and super-snarky at the same time, and has a real talent for art and for blowing huge bubbles of gum in the most menacing way possible. When that big pink bubble **POPS!** in your face, you can bet she's not best pleased with you...

Zed is totally different:

1) he is a boy, which is a bit unexpected, what with St Grizzle's being a girls' school.

2) fact number one might have something to do with him being Lulu's child, along with his sister Swan.

3) unlike the rest of us, he is not lounging on the floor but sitting in his wheelchair.

4) he's wearing these super-cool, neon green PJs that I'm a bit jealous of.

"**Psst!**" Zed hisses at me now.

"What?" I hiss back, frowning up at him.

I don't want to get caught talking – I like Lulu a

lot and don't want her to think I'm rude. And it's not that she's the sort of head teacher who'd give you a month's detention for sneezing in class or anything – she's more likely to look at you with sad, puppy-dog eyes that make you feel totally *terrible* for letting her down, which is worse.

Zed lifts one eyebrow, then holds up a small bag of sweets he's snuck in. Drool...

"So," says Lulu, gazing around at us all and smiling brightly. "Before we move on, does anyone have any thoughts on kindness? Any questions? Yes, Dani?"

Oops. It might have looked like I was starting to put my hand up but I was actually just reaching for a Jelly Baby.

"I ... uh..." I fumble, trying to think fast. "Is the frog all right?" The frog is the reason that today's assembly is about kindness. It's really about kindness to frogs and to dinner ladies.

Yesterday, *someone* put a frog in the kitchen
sink, just before Mrs Hedges – St Grizzle's dinner
lady and housekeeper – went in there to start
making our lunch. Mrs Hedges got a terrible
fright when what looked like an old teabag
jumped up at her. But I think the frog got *more* of
a scare... Mrs Hedges' screams were louder than

the fire alarm that went off last Friday. (The fire
alarm – well, that's another story.)

What I'm going to say next might sound mean
but I think everyone was more worried about the
frog. Mrs Hedges is *not* what you might call
friendly, or cheerful, or fond of children. Swan says
she's allergic to St Grizzle's and everyone in it.

"The frog is fine, thank you, Dani," says Lulu,

with a nod and a bob of her unicorn horn. "Isn't it, Miss Amethyst?"

We all turn round to look at our science and drama teacher, who's wearing a fluffy dressing gown and matching slippers that are the *exact* same shade of purple as her hair, which is currently adorned with curlers. Beside her is Mademoiselle Fabienne (yawning genteely) and Toshio the temporary receptionist, with his headphones round his neck (he can't bear to be parted from his new favourite indie band, even at mealtimes).

Anyway, Lulu's sudden question takes Miss Amethyst a bit by surprise and she chokes a little on her toast and Marmite.

"Yes! The frog was quite all right!" she reassures everyone after a quiet cough. "I took it to the pond in the woods. Perhaps we can do a nature walk as part of biology this week and see how it's doing."

Lots of enthusiastic "Ooh, yes, please!"s echo around the hall, because Miss Amethyst *always* makes her lessons so much fun. On Friday she burned different chemicals to show what amazing colours they'd make while playing an old punky-sounding song called 'Firestarter' really loudly. It was brilliant ... till the fire alarm went off and frightened Twinkle, who went mad. There are two horn-shaped dents in the classroom door where she tried to headbutt her way out.

"Right, let's move on, then!" says Lulu and pulls a piece of paper out of her unicorn pocket.

"I wish she would..." says Swan, who's sitting on the floor next to me.

While Lulu's unfolding the sheet of paper, Zed quickly hands me two Jelly Babies and I just as quickly pass one on to Swan. It might sweeten her up a bit. I've come to realize that she DOES

have a sweet side – it's just that she doesn't

like to show it too often. Sometimes Swan

looks like she's sucked a lemon by

accident and is a little bit furious

about it.

"Exciting news!" Lulu announces,

wafting the sheet of paper at us.

"Bet it's not..." drones Swan.

"THIS is from the local council," Lulu

carries on. "They've emailed all the schools

in the county, asking them to make a short

promotional film about the area. The title of

the project is Why We Love Where We Live.

We can focus on the woods around the school,

or Huddleton, the local village, perhaps."

A film?

My ears prick up as much as my dog

Downboy's at the mention of walkies.

I LOVE making films! Me and my best buddy Arch have shot tons of mini-movies using our ex-toys as actors and posted them on YouTube. I was watching one of our favourites yesterday – our version of *The X Factor* with a Furby, a one-legged Barbie and my T rex as judges, while two Elmers did a rap (yo!).

Apart from Mum and Downboy and my gorgeous Granny Viv, making films with Arch is what I most miss about home...

I clutch my T rex closer (other people sleep with stuffed teddies and rabbits, I have a plastic dinosaur that's been chewed by a goat) and hardly breathe while I wait to hear what Lulu's got to say next.

"The BAD news is, the council haven't given us much time to make our film," says Lulu. "The closing date is the end of the day on Wednesday, so we'll have to get a move on. The GOOD news is, they've invited participating schools to travel to the Town Hall in Dunchester on Friday afternoon for a screening of all the films. Won't that be fun?"

"Mneh," Swan grunts, with a couldn't-care-less shrug of her shoulder.

"And that's not all," Lulu adds. "*After* the screening, the organizers will choose ONE film to feature on the council's new-look website."

"Zzzzzzzzz…" snores Swan.

"And the winning film will get a prize!"

Swan sits up, suddenly interested.

"A prize – like a lot of money, you mean?" she asks.

"It doesn't say," mutters Lulu, scouring the printout in her hand. "But it's not the winning that matters, is it, Swan? It's the taking part that counts!"

Swan makes a sound like a balloon deflating.

But when Lulu speaks next, I feel like I'm about to burst.

"Now, our newest student is, of course, an expert when it comes to making videos. So I suggest that Dani Dexter should be our director."

And I blush so much when everyone cheers that I worry the heat from my face will set off the fire alarm again. Wait till I tell Arch!

"And as fellow Fungi and the oldest students, I think Zed and Swan should be part of the production team, alongside Dani," Lulu declares.

Me and Zed do a high five.

I turn round and go to do the same to Swan but she gives me a don't-even-think-about-it stare and I pretend to smooth my hair instead.

"But, remember, it's a whole-school project, guys," Lulu says to the three of us. "So I want you to find a role for everyone. Cos at St Grizelda's, we're a team. Isn't that right, **CONKERS!**"

"Yes!" call out the ten-year-old Conkers.

"Aren't we, **OTTERS!**"

The nine-year-old triplets, who hardly ever speak, nod enthusiastically.

"Aren't we, **NEWTS!**"

"**YEAHHHHHH!**" roar a whole bunch of eight-year-olds with peanut-butter-and-Marmite-smeared hands, faces and PJs.

"Um, Ms Murphy?" says Yas.

Yas isn't in PJs; she's the only pupil who still wears the old school uniform of grey skirt and stripey tie. Yas doesn't call our head teacher Lulu either – she still calls her Ms Murphy. Yas is lovely but she thinks the new-look St Grizelda's is completely bonkers and is waiting for her dad to come and collect her. She says he'll be here any day. But the truth of it is, she's been saying that for two months.

"Yes, Yas?" says Lulu.

"Um, not all of the Newts are here..."

Lulu frowns. Everyone stares at the Newts, and they stare back at us as we count them.

"One, two, three, four, five, six, seven..." Lulu says aloud. "We're missing three!"

Three, which includes Blossom, who's part-child, part-goblin. And who everyone reckons is responsible for the frog-sink-dinner-lady-freak-out yesterday...

"Er, Lulu," says May-Belle, kneeling up in her bat-patterned PJs and pointing towards the big windows that overlook the garden.

"Maybe they're out there, with that ghost?"

GHOST!

GHOST!

You have never seen seventeen children, four adults and a goat move quicker.

We reach the windows in a rackety jumble, only to see a shrouded white figure careering across the lawn, screeeechhhhing like a ... a screechy thing.

Looks like St Grizzle's School for Girls, Goats and Random Boys has a new – and unwelcome – guest.

Gulp...

Chapter 2
Great Minds DON'T Think Alike

And huffy farewells...

We're all completely terrified for about two and a half seconds.

Then – as we stare at the flappity-flapping white figure – super-sensible Yas says something super-sensible.

"Ms Murphy, isn't that the big net curtain that's usually *here*?"

Yas points first at the "ghost" and then at the net-free window we're staring out of. Everyone looks up and around, wondering where the curtain's gone, as well as the ones from the rest of the grand windows in the hall.

"You know something?" Lulu says thoughtfully. "I DID ask Mrs Hedges to give them a wash..."

"So, do you think *that's* Mrs Hedges?" I ask, nodding out at the wailing "ghost" that's just narrowly avoided running into a tree.

"I think you might be right, Dani," says Lulu, with a horn-bobbing nod.

I'm sure I *am* right. Apart from anything else, I've just noticed that the "ghost" is wearing brown Crocs. It would be a bit of a coincidence if a real ghost happened to have the same taste in footwear as St Grizzle's only dinner lady.

"Maybe the curtain blew *off* the washing line and *on to* Mrs Hedges when she was hanging it up?" Zed suggests.

Zed is a really, *really* nice, kind person. So he's wondering if Mrs Hedges getting entangled in a large layer of wispy white material is an accident. Meanwhile, it's dawning on the rest of us that it isn't the case.

"OK, where are they?" sighs Lulu, staring out at the garden for trouble.

Trouble in the shape of Blossom and her two escapee Newt buddies, she means, who we've all worked out have something to do with the "ghost".

Swan spots them first and points at the

nearest old oak tree.

I squint, like everyone else, and suddenly see them – three goblinish girls, huddled on their haunches high up in the branches.

Swan throws opens the window – and the sound of sniggering drifts in. Now we all know where to look, it's plain to see that the girls are holding a messy bundle that looks suspiciously like another of the stolen-from-the-laundry-basket net curtains, ready to be dropped on whichever unsuspecting person or goat might pass by.

"Oi!" Swan yells at them. "You lot are SO busted! Get in here, NOW!"

The first reaction to Swan's yell is that the other bundled curtain gets dumped and flumps down on to the grass. The second reaction comes in the shape of a flurry of rustling leaves and shaking branches, as Blossom and co start clambering down from the tree.

"Not *quite* how I'd have put it, Swan, darling," says Lulu, though she's pulling down the hood of her onesie, like she means business. "But thank you. Now, while I deal with these girls, can the rest of you go and get dressed and ready for the day?"

The drama as well as the assembly is over, so we all begin to move away from the window, picking up our duvets and pillows and dragging them out of the hall.

"Uh ... do you think maybe someone should rescue Madame Hedges?" we hear Mademoiselle Fabienne say hesitantly in her pretty French accent, as we hear another wail from outside.

There are a few "mmm"s and "suppose so"s, and then everyone carries on to their dorms.

Monday's first class is circus skills, which is a whole-school lesson with Lulu – at least it's supposed to be. But we've all been hovering out on the back lawn for *ages*, wondering where Lulu is. Finally she shows up, holding a steaming mug in each hand.

"That smells **AWFUL!**" roars Blossom. "Like WET STRAW from a STABLE!"

"It's camomile tea and it's very calming," says Lulu, who's changed out of her unicorn onesie and into her sensible work clothes, i.e. a T-shirt with the logo of some ancient punk rock band on it, a pair of raggedy-fringed shorts and orange flip-flops.

"Um ... do we have to juggle with them?" asks one of the Newts, staring at the mugs and looking worried.

"No, they're not to do with the circus skills class. They're drinks for me and Mrs Hedges. We're going to have a little chat in my office and talk about what happened earlier," Lulu replies, fixing her gaze on Blossom and her two partners in crime. "Have you girls done what I asked? Have you written Mrs Hedges a 'sorry' letter?"

"Yes." Blossom nods hard, her birds' nest of hair bobbing earnestly. "It is a really LOVELY and NICE sorry letter. We stuck it on the fridge."

"Good," says Lulu. "Well, while I have this chat with Mrs Hedges, can all of you amuse yourselves quietly and productively? Maybe you could start discussing ideas for the short film competition? I won't be long!"

Amusing ourselves quietly and productively ... it's a nice thought but as soon as Lulu disappears inside, everyone scampers off like puppies lolloping after balls.

So much for discussing ideas for the short film but I guess that can wait. There's something I'm itching to do...

Ten minutes later, I'm out on the front lawn with a gaggle of girls and a random boy and the elegant stone statue of St Grizelda watching over us – or to give her her less-than-elegant nickname, St Grizzle.

A mysterious someone – no one knows who – regularly likes to style St Grizzle in new and interesting ways. Today she is wearing a shower cap and has a pine cone and a banana in her outstretched hands.

Maybe it's because the shower cap is practically over her eyes but St Grizzle looks a bit puzzled by what we're up to.

Last night, while I was curled up in my bunk in the huge but mostly empty Fungi dorm, I had the idea of doing a mini-movie especially for Mum. Every time I talk to her, she bangs on about all the things she's missing in the Antarctic. Those things include:

1) me
2) Granny Viv
3) Hobnobs and
4) *green*.

"It's so WHITE here!" she said when she FaceTimed me yesterday. She turned the phone around so I could see all the snow and ice and the total whitey-whiteness.

So, to remind Mum of home, I am now filming a rolling GREEN English field with a herd of cows making their way across it.

Sort of.

Well, OK – I don't have time to find a handy rolling English field and a herd of cows, so instead there's a bunch of potatoes with googly eyes on the school's front lawn.

Yaz and Blossom helped by sticking the eyes on the "cows", i.e. the potatoes the triplets just "borrowed" from the school kitchen while Mrs Hedges is holed up in Lulu's office.

"Yep, that's about right," I say to Klara and Angel, who've been carefully placing the spud herd on a patch of grass. I'm directing them as I lie on my tummy, holding my phone sideways to film. "And ready to move them again?"

I'm shooting a rehearsal just now – we'll use proper stop-frame animation for the final version, where, bit by bit, the "cows" will meander across the grass.

"Moo!" says Zed, practising the sound effects I'm going to add later.

"Excellent," I tell him as I watch Klara and Angel position the potatoes.

"Uh-oh!" I hear Swan call out from the tyre swing. "Incoming GOAT!"

Too late – four giant legs have already appeared in the frame. And before anyone can shoo Twinkle away she sniffs first at the camera, then at the lead actor potato, before –

* CRUNCH! * – happily munching it between her yellow teeth.

"Stop! Stop!" I yell, waving my hands at Twinkle. She takes precisely no notice and helps herself to another spud.

As I go to turn off my
phone, I hear *another* sound
– my schoolfriends howling
with laughter.

So I stay where I am and
keep filming.

After all, a giant goat photobombing a tiny potato cow herd
might get me my *best ever* hit-rate
on YouTube! Though it's going to be
hard to beat the 903 hits I got last
Sunday, when Newts Class decided it was WAY
too long to wait till winter and I filmed them
covering the statue of St Grizzle with squirty
cream snow.

Twinkle finishes her potato snack, has a little
burp and trots off stage left.

* CUT! *

I shuffle up on to my knees eager to check

the footage and see that May-Belle has wandered over from the front steps of the school, where she has been taking selfies in one of her fabulously gloomy, goth-y black outfits. And a whole bunch of Newts have appeared out of nowhere, curious to know what's going on/ being destroyed by Twinkle.

That means we're ALL here, the entire teeny-tiny school. So maybe – just like Lulu suggested – we should have a quick meeting about the Why We Love Where We Live film project!

I feel a sudden flurry of excitement. Me and Arch always came up with excellent ideas for our mini-movies and had such good fun putting them together. And that was just two of us – imagine how awesome it's going to be working with everyone at school!

"Hey, how about we have a bit of a meeting about the film idea?" I suggest.

Everyone perks up like meerkats, even Swan, who never likes to show she's particularly excited about anything. She blows and **POPS!** the pink bubblegum she's been chewing, then unhooks her long, skinny legs from the tyre swing and comes on over, joining everyone else on the lawn.

Ooh, it's quite exciting having everyone looking at me like I'm the Boss!

"Cool!" says May-Belle. "So, what's our idea? And how do we decide who does what?"

I haven't had much of a chance to think it through, since we only found out about the film project twenty-seven minutes ago and for most of those twenty-seven minutes I've been getting dressed, brushing my teeth and filming potato cows. But now's the time to get going...

"Well," I begin, "I'm the director, and—"

"—and me and Zed are part of the production team," Swan interrupts.

"Uh-huh, yeah, sure," I say quickly as my brain whirrs with planning. "Anyway, cos I've done a lot of filming in the past, I'll also be the main cameraman. But I thought Zed would be a great second cameraman, since he can zoom in and out of shots really smoothly, if someone pushes his chair."

Zed grins and punches the air.

Yas also has her hand in the air but in more of a polite, question-asking sort of way.

"Yes?" I say to her, suddenly feeling cool and in control, like I'm a teacher.

"Who'll be the presenter or voiceover person?" Yas asks.

"Um, I suppose *I'll* do it," I say. "I've done plenty of voices for characters in the mini-movies I've made with my friend Arch."

Yas purses her lips, like she's imagining the range of voices I can do.

"Scuse me, Dani, but what about editing?" asks Angel, waving her hand in the air now, the thin metal bracelets on her wrists jingle-jangling.

I'm impressed that Angel has thought about the editing part of filming as that's really important. Not that she'll know how it works, of course.

"Yeah, I guess I'd better do that, too," I say, "since I've had so much practice AND I have an app for editing on my phone."

I notice a bunch of whispering and hubbubbing going on, some between the triplets of Otter Class and some among Blossom and the rest of her Newt gang. They all seem really excited about this project!

It's Klara's turn to put her hand up next.

"So, Dani, you're directing and filming and presenting and editing," she says with a little frown of her white-blond eyebrows, like she's trying to make sure she's got her facts right.

"Er, yes, I suppose so..." I reply, feeling a little wriggle of something in my tummy all of a sudden. The sort of wriggle when you realize you might have got something a bit wrong. Klara doesn't think I've been bossy, or grabbed all the good jobs for myself, does she? I haven't *meant* it that way ... I just have more experience than everyone else, which is why Lulu put me in charge.

"Then what are the *rest* of us going to be doing?" Klara asks, blinking at me with her so-pale-they're-practically-invisible eyelashes.

Uh-oh – I think she DOES think I've been bossy and grabbed all the good jobs for myself. And the way everyone else is staring at me, they might be starting to think that way, too. Maybe *that's* what all the whispering and hubbubbing was about.

"Well, um ... someone will need to push Zed when it's his turn to film stuff!" I suggest, knowing that probably sounds a bit lame.

"So, while you're doing everything, Dani, the rest of us just have to take turns pushing Zed around…?" says May-Belle.

Uh-oh. May-Belle looks nearly as grumpy as the skull and crossbones on her T-shirt.

Yikes! I've only ever made films with Arch, and we've made so many that we just get on with it, him doing the stuff *he's* good at, me doing the stuff *I'm* good at.

This is totally different. How am I supposed to be in charge of ALL these people and find enough jobs for everyone?

And I can't think properly and fix this with all the not-very-whispery whispers going on, especially now that the Conkers have joined in.

"I'VE got an idea, Dani Dexterer!" yelps Blossom, waving her (dirty) hand around madly. "How about each class does its OWN filming around the school and the woods and the village and you just put them all together in the editing thingy at the end?"

"Yeah, but it might not match up very well if they're all filmed separately and—"

My protests are out-whooped by the Newts, who then – in the blink of an eye – slink off into the bushes as if they were never there.

The triplets stare at each other and quietly slope off, too, which I presume means they like Blossom's idea.

"Sounds kind of fun," says Yas, nodding around at the other three Conkers. May-Belle, Klara and Angel nod back, uncross their legs and meander away with Yas, while I watch, stunned.

POP! goes one of Swan's bubbles and she narrows her almond eyes in my direction.

"Well, THAT went well!" she says. "So much for us all working together, as a team..."

Her cool glower says it all. I messed up the project and everyone is cross with me.

Well, maybe not sweet, lovely Zed. He holds his hand down to me and I take it, hurtling myself up into a standing position.

JUST as I'm about to thank him for his small kindness, I see Mrs Hedges stomping down the front steps of the school, with her jacket on and a bag jammed full of kitchen paraphernalia.

"Goodbye and good riddance!" she calls out,

crunching across the stones of the driveway, only pausing long enough to grab the banana out of St Grizzle's hand. "You're all mad, the lot of you!"

Mrs Hedges speeds up as Twinkle goes hurtling after her and/or the banana.

"**Arrgghhhhhh!**" we hear her yell as she disappears out of the school grounds and – presumably – out of our lives.

"Bye, Mrs Hedges," I mutter sadly.

I am muttering sadly because, like the other pupils at St Grizzle's, although we will not miss Mrs Hedges – or her grumps – we will miss her cooking. (Cooking that's ALMOST as yummy as my fab Granny Viv's.)

RIP Mrs Hedges' lasagne and sticky toffee pudding.

Chapter 3
Wibbles, Spigots and Whoopsies

And cowboy whoops...

When Mum first dropped me off at St Grizzle's, I was so homesick it hurt as badly as getting hit in the chest with the ball during a game of rounders.

Then I got to know – and like – every oddball here.

So, yes, after a bumpy start, I realized I really, truly, definitely liked it at St Grizzle's and would be very happy to stay here for the three months that Mum's away.

Till this morning.

Thing is, I've got a bad case of the Homesick Wibbles again. I think that's because:

1) for the first time ever, I'm failing at what I do best – making mini-movies. Lulu has put me in charge of the Why We Love Where We Live project, and even before I've got started it's turned into an #epicfail.

2) in the space of about two minutes, I managed to irritate all my new schoolmates

and everyone has given up on me and is doing their own thing.

3) there is no more of Mrs Hedges' comforting almost-like-Granny-Viv's home cooking...

And so I've scooted up to the vast Fungi dorm room – which I share with only Swan – in search of a familiar voice...

"No reply from Mum," I tell my small T rex, who's lying on the bed beside me. He needs his rest these days – his tail and leg are a bit mangled after Twinkle mistook him for a snack.

It's no surprise I can't get hold of Mum. The reception's not great out in the vast snowy expanses of the Antarctic, funnily enough. She can only check in when she's back at base camp and not busy analyzing penguin-bottom data.

I flop back on my bunk, where the big T rex – the huge mural that Swan spray-painted on the wall – looms over me.

"There's no point calling Arch, is there? Not when he's in school," I say to it.

If either T rex could talk, I'm sure they'd tell me who I should call next – but I'm already on it.

I scroll through my contacts and press dial. The call is answered. Sort of.

"   "

"Hello?" I say, wondering why no one is talking.

"   "

"GRANNY VIV?" I say loudly, into the silence.

Then I finally hear something from the other end … a noisy **thunk-a-thunk** and **DUH-DUH-DUH** and then a big ***sigh***.

"Sorry, Dani – I've put you on speakerphone. Just having a bit of a nightmare with the engine here."

"What's wrong with the Mini?" I ask her. Granny Viv's car is very old, very rusty and the same pillar-box red as her hair.

"Hold on... Nearly got it..." Granny Viv says distractedly, probably because she's concentrating on wrenching a spigot or spigotting a wrench or something, rather than talking to me.

"Hmm, not sure if that's worked," I hear Granny Viv say with another sigh. "Anyway, how are you, darling?"

"Fine. Well, fine-*ish*. You see—"

Brooooom, BROOOOOOOM! BROOOOOOOOOMMM! "Yee-HA!"

Before I can launch into my moan, I'm interrupted by the deafening roar of an engine and Granny Viv doing a triumphant cowboy whoop.

This is almost immediately followed first by a **chuggetty PUTT-putt-putt** noise as the engine dies again and then by a disappointed, "Oh."

The assorted car noises and cowboy yelps have obviously sent Downboy mad – I can hear him "**ARF! ARF! ARF!**"ing his head off, and have to take the phone away from the side of my head so I don't end up with a burst eardrum.

"Look, can I call you back in a bit, sweetpea?" I *just* about make out Granny Viv saying. "It's all a bit chaotic here at the minute. Anyway, don't you have lessons? Shouldn't you be dangling from a trapeze in the garden or learning to juggle or something?"

"I'll explain later," I tell her, hoping I don't sound too disappointed at not being able to chat.

There's a loud ***CLANG!*** at Granny Viv's end, which sounds a little bit like she's hitting the car with a hammer, so I end the call and flump back on to the bed, just as the dorm door thwacks open.

"All right?" says Swan, padding over and sitting beside me on my bunk.

I settle back on my bed and shake my head.

"Not really," I mumble. "I totally messed up that meeting about the film and made everyone cross with me."

"Well, not *everyone*," says Swan, giving me hope once I spot the little smirk on her face.

"I didn't make you cross?" I say, feeling brighter.

"Oh, yeah, you *definitely* made me cross," she says, not mincing her words. "I mean, did you forget that me and Zed are meant to be part of the production team? That we're supposed to help you make plans and decisions?"

"Er ... sorry. I just got carried away. And ... and I don't know what I'm doing," I admit.

"Fair enough. Just as well you've got a

fantastic production team, isn't it?"

Swan raises one eyebrow as she blows a huge pink bubble.

"What about the others?" I ask. "You said not everyone is cross?"

POP! goes the bubble.

"Well, Zed's not cross," Swan replies, winding the gum around her finger. "But that's cos he's excited about being the second cameraman. And the Newts and the Otters aren't cross – they're just excited about goofing around filming stuff on their phones."

"And the Conkers?" I ask hesitantly.

"Oh, yeah, they were *all* cross," Swan says with a casual shrug. "But I've talked to them, and they'll be OK. They're just annoyed you didn't seem to want to listen to them."

"What were they trying to tell me?" I ask, feeling confused.

"OK, for a start, Yas was keen to do the presenting or voiceover stuff," Swan begins, "cos her dad is a diplomat and she's heard him do a ton of speeches over the years."

"Oh, right..." I mumble.

I feel particularly guilty about Yas. Until I showed her my mini-movies, she wasn't into any of the arty-crafty classes of the new-look St Grizzle's. She's definitely loosened up since then, and the other day she even put down her maths book and joined in making a full-sized igloo out of empty plastic milk containers in art.

"And Angel would've liked to try editing," Swan carries on. "Her mum's a famous Bollywood actress and Angel's been behind the scenes on loads of her films."

"Ah…" I mumble some more.

With that useful knowledge, I can see why Angel would want to volunteer herself and why she'd be grumpy with me for not letting her explain.

"May-Belle wanted to ask about maybe doing some background music. Her parents are country music singers from Nashville in America," says Swan. "They're on a big world tour at the moment."

"Mmm…" I mumble yet again.

Some upbeat guitar music might've been nice to add but I don't think mini-goth May-Belle has the same musical tastes as her guitar-strumming mum and dad. "What about Klara?" I ask.

"What do *her* parents do?"

"They're both super-brainy professors from Germany," Swan explains. "They're always away at conferences around the world."

Huh. I try to imagine ditzy, daydreamy Klara with brainiac parents but my own brain stalls.

"What did *she* want to do for the film project?" I ask, wondering how I let Klara down as well.

"Klara just wondered if she could do some cartwheels in the film, cos she's very proud of the fact that she can do six in a row…" says Swan, rolling her eyes. "Anyway, you've just missed assembly."

"I have? Another one? But I've only been up here a few minutes!" I protest.

"It was pretty quick – Lulu just announced that Mrs Hedges has left, and that we'll all have to pitch in with the cooking and cleaning till she finds a replacement. She spotted you weren't there though and asked me to come get you," says Swan, who's already up and heading off out of the dorm.

"Why does she want to see me?" I ask, following her out into the corridor and down the stairs.

Out of the long window, I can see Miss Amethyst on the back lawn. She's wafting about in her usual elegant, purple layers while pegging up lots and lots and lots of pairs of pants on the washing line. She's obviously getting stuck in with the helping-out duties already.

"Don't ask me. I never know what's going on in my mother's mind," Swan says casually as we come to the bottom of the staircase and see Toshio sliding across the hall tiles with dusters tied around his hi-top trainers.

"I skitter and floor get clean, yes?" he says, holding his thumbs up.

Toshio is a Japanese student who's taken on the job of temporary receptionist at St Grizzle's in exchange for English lessons. Sadly, he's not very good at either working or English yet.

"Er, I think you mean *skate*," I correct him as we pass but he can't hear cos of the music blaring in his headphones.

I hurry along the right-hand corridor after Swan, and soon we're sinking into the beanbags Lulu keeps in her office for visitors. Zed is already here, parked by Lulu's desk.

"Well, what an action-packed morning!" says Lulu, from the comfort of her swivelly chair.

Behind her is the spray-painted rainforest mural that Swan did to brighten up the room. From this angle, it looks like a toucan is pecking at Lulu's head.

"So, Dani," she says, slapping her hands on the desk. "Swan and Zed have told me that the first film meeting went a bit ... whoopsie."

"Whoopsie?" I repeat in a small, uncertain voice.

"You know…" says Lulu, tumbling her hands in the air and pulling an "erk!" sort of face.

Actually, that IS a very good way to describe the meeting.

"But all I wanted to say was that having things go whoopsie and then sorting them out is an important Life Skill," says Lulu.

Ah, Lulu is big on Life Skills and how to learn from them, the way my old head teacher was big on detention if you forgot your PE kit.

"So, I just want you to have a rethink, Dani," says Lulu, "and then get back on with this project, because I have every faith in you! OK?"

"OK," I repeat, blushing quite a lot. Being told someone has faith in you is really quite, well, blushy stuff.

"Good! Great! So any of you young brainboxes got suggestions as to how I can find a new Mrs Hedges?" Lulu asks with a hopeful smile, staring round at the three of us.

"You don't think Mrs Hedges will change her mind then, Mum?" asks Zed. "Maybe if she goes home and cools off..."

"Sadly, she sounded very, VERY sure that she's had enough," says Lulu. "And look what she did to Blossom and the girls' apology!"

Frowning sadly, Lulu picks up two torn halves of a letter from her desk.

Put together, they read:

Deer Mrs Hedges -
We are VERY sorry for
if it was a bit funy.
Love, Newts

being numpties, even

"They put a lot of thought into it, too," says Lulu. "Look at all the decoration!"

Hmm. There does seem to be more decoration than actual apology in the letter. It's covered in glued-on spangles and feathers and coloured teeny pom-poms.

"Well, we should be OK for a while. I mean, you know everyone will help out, right?" says Swan.

"Yes, but what if it goes on for weeks, and ... oh dear, I'm not sure what to do first!" Lulu sighs, her shoulders sinking down. (So it's not just ME having a bad morning.) "There doesn't seem much in the fridge or kitchen cupboards for a start."

"Well, then, YOU'RE going to get on to the supermarket website and put in a food order," Swan says matter-of-factly. "If you do it quickly, they might be able to deliver it tonight."

"Yes! Put in a food order, deliver it tonight,

fingers crossed," Lulu repeats, perking up and pulling her laptop towards her. "But what about lunch?"

"Me, Zed and Dani could go into the village and buy a whole load of pizzas," says Swan. "And at the same time, we can scout around Huddleton for good spots to use in our Why We Love Where We Live film. Is that OK, Dani?"

"Um, sure," I agree, happy that one of the production team has had an actual idea.

"Perfect!" says Lulu. "But I'm meant to be teaching circus skills, not doing online shopping. What about the Conkers, Otters and Newts?"

"They want to scout around on their own," says Swan. "I'll tell them that they can only go as far as the school grounds and the woods beyond and have to stick together in their classes. What's Mademoiselle Fabienne doing now?"

"The breakfast dishes," says Lulu.

"Well, why don't you ask her and Miss Amethyst to oversee them, since filming is artistic and wandering around the grounds and the woods is practically a nature study lesson."

Lulu blinks at her daughter in wonder and awe.

"Swan Chen-Murphy, you really will be Prime Minister one day," she tells her.

Instead of blushing like me, Swan blows a giant "whatever" pink bubble of gum.

POP!

Chapter 4
Meeting Meanie McMeanpants

And not being bothered...

We should've probably done our scouting-for-locations BEFORE we did our shopping.

Zed has two big bags of pizza dangling from each handle of his wheelchair while me and Swan carry two more each. And mine keep whacking against my legs with every step. ***ouch!***

We should've left Twinkle at home, too, or at least found her a muzzle – she's not fussed that the pizzas are frozen and keeps trying to nibble them through the bags. But then again, maybe she just enjoys the taste of plastic.

"It's just down here," says Zed, who wants us to check out an interesting old bridge across the river that's kind of, well, interesting and old.

I sigh – not because it's not a good suggestion, but because its dawning on me that we only have till the end of the day on Wednesday to put a film together. And the way we're going, we won't have anything to submit at all...

Swan hears the sigh sneak out.

"Why are you all gloomy around the edges?" she asks. "We'll find some locations today, OK?"

"Well, that would be great," I tell her. "But how do we get all the Conkers, Otters and Newts back on board? How do we make it a team effort if they're all off shooting their own random films?"

"Don't worry, Dani," she reassures me. "Their films will not just be random, they will be rubbish without a director to organize everything. But let them get it out of their systems. We'll watch all their films together tonight and then when everyone sees how bad they are, we'll tell them what we're REALLY going to do!"

"Including giving them proper jobs to do on the project," I add, now I've learned my lesson.

"And by then we'll have chosen all these

amazing locations from around the village," says Zed, turning down a side street.

This side street isn't too amazing. It's pretty ugly, actually, with rows of small industrial units crouched behind an ugly metal fence.

We passed quite a few not-terrifically-lovely buildings on our way into the village as well – a concrete car park, a doctor's surgery that looked like the architect had based it on the shoebox of his trainers and a new block of flats with tiny windows that reminded me of a documentary I once saw about prisons. Maybe all this ugly modern stuff was why the local council wanted to try and remind people of the nice parts of the area that still exist.

"Uh-oh…" groans Zed, and he begins to slow his wheels.

"Great…" snarls Swan.

OK, now I see what they do. A pretty, tree-lined river, a historic and very scenic bridge – and a bunch of kids from the village school.

A bunch of kids I've come across once before, on my first visit to the village a couple of weeks ago. This lot were so Meanie McMeanpants that I wasn't in a desperate hurry to see them again.

"Hey, *look*, everyone!" says a tall boy with a floppy blond quiff and a clipboard. "It's some smelly Grizzlers!"

I remember what his name is – Spencer. His little gang, in their black and green Huddleton school uniform, snigger like he's a comedy genius.

Swan keeps walking straight towards them, staring them out, blowing the biggest I-don't-care pink bubble imaginable. Me and Zed shyly pad and roll behind her.

"So, what are you doing here? Let me guess?" says Spencer, tapping a pen against his lip and doing a comic-book exaggerated frown.

"Hmm... Looking for places to shoot your Why We Love Where We Live film. Right?"

"Maybe," Swan says with a shrug. "So what?"

"So," Spencer suddenly sneers at her, "you can't film the bridge. WE got here first. AND we're doing the market cross, the old church, the duck pond on the green and the WWI memorial. EVIDENCE."

Spencer holds up the clipboard, and we can see some scribbled notes on it.

"Now we've decided on our locations, we're coming back tomorrow to do our filming, using the school's BRAND-NEW VIDEO CAMERA, then editing it on the school's BRAND-NEW EDITING SOFTWARE, so don't even think about doing the same stuff, cos we're going to nail it. OK, losers?"

I shuffle closer to Zed and I think he'd shuffle closer to me, only that's quite a complicated back-and-forth manoeuvre in a wheelchair.

Swan **POPs!** her ginormous bubble, which makes snidey Spencer and his gang of twonks jerk in surprise.

"You think we're bothered?" she says, once she's wrapped the pink strands of gum around her finger and sucked the whole lot back in her mouth with a defiant slurp. "We only came this way cos we were walking the goat. We have LOADS of better location ideas than *this*…"

Swan spins round effortlessly on her heel, her waist-length black hair flipping behind her, and begins to walk off, giving a casual tug at Twinkle's extendable lead.

Passing me and Zed she winks, and we both immediately try and turn just a *fraction* as coolly as she did.

"What location ideas do we have that are so much better?" Zed hisses at his sister as we catch her up.

"We don't – yet," Swan replies, as if finding prize-winning locations is as easy as opening a bag of crisps.

"No! Gerroff! Give that back! Oi...!" I hear Spencer yell behind us.

I nearly turn around to see what's up but then Twinkle clatters up beside us and contentedly falls into step with our walk. Chewing on a clipboard.

"Bring it on..." I say with a grin as a little bubble of possibility and excitement fizzles inside me once again.

Chapter 5
And the Award for Most Rubbish Film Goes to...

And Brussels sprout mash...

We had a "surprise" tea this evening.

With no supermarket delivery slot available till later tomorrow, Lulu and Toshio had to get inventive, cooking every single food item they could find in our nearly empty cupboards and freezer.

No one had the same thing – we each just got a plate of randomness handed to us. Mine was a fish finger and spring onion sandwich, Swan's was baked bean and corned beef hash and Zed ended up with cauliflower cheese on toast. It was a **LOT** of fun, especially when we had a vote about whose was the most disgusting. One of the triplets won with her burnt bacon 'n' Brussels sprout mash.

And now tea's over and the dishes are done and put away, it's time for the film showings. Everyone's gathered in the art classroom, from Lulu the head right down to the smallest Newt.

Yas suggested we do the screening in here because Mademoiselle Fabienne has a really big, deliciously soft, fluffy rug on the floor in front of her whiteboard to sit on.

She also has flowers in a vase on her desk, plus a pretty fringed lamp and some framed photos of Antoine, her pet lizard back home in France. It's very cosy and relaxing, especially with all the artwork up on the walls.

Though the thudding of Twinkle's horns on the other side of the door is *kind* of distracting. Still, she has to understand that bad behaviour has consequences. Until Twinkle learns that it's plain *wrong* to eat teachers' shoes and random art supplies, she's banned.

"Turn the lights off!" someone shouts out

and Blossom jumps up to flick a few switches, leaving it *just* bright enough for me to see what I'm doing at the computer, under the fringed lamp's soft glow.

It feels strange being in charge of school equipment, while actual teachers are sitting on chairs in the back row. But it would probably have taken grown-ups like Lulu, Mademoiselle Fabienne and Miss Amethyst five years to figure out how to download the vids the younger classes had filmed on their phones on to Mademoiselle Fabienne's laptop.

I guess Toshio might have managed, since he's about eighteen and is technocentric but he's been too busy serving up mugs of sugary popcorn to everyone to go with the evening's entertainment.

"OK, so here's film number one, from the Conkers!" I announce.

Once the pop-concert-level shrieking and yelling ebbs away, I hit **PLAY**.

And up pops Yas – "It's YAS!" squeals a Newt – on the whiteboard. Yas is standing beside the statue of St Grizzle, who's been tidied up for filming and is no longer sporting a shower cap and clutching a pine cone.

Some music starts. It's dark and grungy-sounding. The camera turns a little to the right and we see May-Belle holding up a novelty mini-speaker in the shape of a panda's head.

"No, Klara! Don't turn it on me!" May-Belle hisses, and the phone gets roughly shoved back round to face Yas.

"Hi, there!" says Yas, holding a microphone to her mouth, though on closer squinting, I see from the shape of it that it might be a tube of sweets that's been covered in tinfoil. "We love where we live – quite literally. Because *we* are lucky enough to go to school in this incredible building, which must be one of the most beautiful in the area. St Grizelda's School for Girls is over a hundred years old and its first ever head teacher, Miss Augusta Wilberbuttle, had this to say about it..."

Up till now, apart from the pretty gloomy music, the Conkers' vid has *almost* gone all right, especially since it's obvious that Yas has done some research. She now holds up a piece of paper and begins to read.

"*Every girl who walks into the hallowed hallways of St Grizelda's will be treated as an individual. Because at St Grizelda's, we believe that girls should be as free to grow as the trees in the woods that surround us. A St Grizelda girl will be valued. Her talents will be appreciated, whatever they may—*"

New music blasts in suddenly, Bollywood-style bhangra, which is MUCH louder than May-Belle's gloomy goth tune. The camera moves round to the left, where Angel – in the most glorious pink-and-gold-beaded *sari* – puts a large boom box down on the grass and begins to dance.

Her dancing is brilliant but above the music you can hear a cross-sounding Yas yelling, "Not yet! Not yet, Angel!".

And then the camera goes all wobbly and there's Klara, excitedly hissing, "Here, take it – take it!" and May-Belle answering, "But this isn't

what we decided!" before the camera is lifted and straightened again and Klara is caught merrily cartwheeling past Angel, while Yas holds her head in her hands.

The film ends.

"**Hurray! Yay!**" yell all the Newts, who I think have all had extra sugar on their popcorn. (I'm pretty sure the bump under Blossom's T-shirt when she came in was the sugar bowl from the kitchen.)

As for the Conkers, they're all looking a bit sheepish after the screening, to be honest.

"I was meant to finish reading out Miss Wilberbuttle's words, and then introduce Angel and Klara," Yas starts to explain. "But everything got a bit rushed..."

I peek at Swan across a darkened room, and just make out her giving me a subtle "told-you!" eyebrow raise.

So far, she's been so right. It's all going horribly, brilliantly wrong.

On to the next film...

"Next, we have the Otters," I say, "telling – I mean, *showing* us what is so special about where we live..."

Cue more crazy yells from the Newts as I press PLAY again.

The triplets must have their phone propped up on a branch, because all three of them are standing facing the camera, in a clearing in the woods.

There is no musical background.

No grungy tunes, no bhangra beats.

There is no presenter, with or without a pretend microphone. No one talks. No one moves.

The triplets just stare at the camera, while some crows squawk-squawk menacingly in the distance.

It's pretty creepy. In fact, it's pretty creepy for about two whole minutes – which feels like quite a long time when you're being creeped out – till Lulu cheerfully shouts out, "How wonderfully atmospheric! But how about stopping it there so we can see what the Newts have been up to?"

I can't tell how the sitting-here-now triplets feel about their film being cut short (and I know it runs to nearly *ten* minutes, since I checked when I uploaded it), as they are just staring at themselves – freeze-framed – on screen.

I risk a quick peek at Zed, who gives me a double thumbs up, then seems to think that people might spot him and changes it into a fake popcorn-stuck-in-the-throat cough.

Quickly, I flip to our last film. The Newts.

They give themselves the BIGGEST cheer yet, and look round at Miss Amethyst, who went out with them while they did their filming.

Miss Amethyst claps madly while they grin at her but as soon as they all turn back to gawp at the screen, she slaps her forehead and has to be comforted by Mademoiselle Fabienne.

PLAY

The first image is of a big, blurry nostril.

"You'll have to step back further than THAT, Blossom," we hear Miss Amethyst say.

The big, blurry nostril moves, and turns into

a big, blurry nose.

"Further," Miss Amethyst orders.

"HA HA HA HA HA HA HA!"
cackles Blossom,
retreating fast, so
that the nose
becomes a crazed-
eyed face.

HA HA

HA HA HA HA

A gaggle of Newts
are behind her,
holding their hands
to their faces as they snigger.

"So," says Miss Amethyst from behind the
phone's camera. "Why don't you girls tell us what's
so special about this wonderful old oak here?"

The only response is ten Newts disappearing
up a tree.

"Girls?" Miss Amethyst says, after a moment
or two.

There's no answer, apart from giggles, and no sign of the Newts, apart from twenty dangling bare feet.

"Well, time for a cup of tea, I think…" mutters Miss Amethyst and the screen goes blank.

"**YEAH! WAHHH!**" go the Newts as the overhead lights flick back on.

Lulu is standing by the switch, smiling enthusiastically. I wonder what she's going to say. Swan has already had a word with her mum about the filming mutiny.

"What SUPER first attempts, everyone!" she announces. "Really different and interesting takes on the project. But I was just thinking, maybe it would be even better if we all took a step back and left the films with Dani to mull over, since she's the director."

I hear a sharp cough coming from the direction of Swan and instantly realize it translates as "Quick! Now's your chance to say something positive!".

"Um, yes! I'd love to watch the films again—"

Another sharp cough.

"—with my production team of Swan and Zed," I add quickly, "and see how we might use all your skills in the final version. If, er, that's OK."

"Well, that sounds more than OK to me!" Lulu enthuses. "How about it, everyone?"

There's a moment's silence, where I half expect someone to mutter "Nah!" out loud. But there are no "Nah"s. There's only a whole lot of jumbled "Yeah!"s, "OK!"s and "Whee!"s.

"Good stuff," says Lulu. "Well, what an eventful day it's been. So how about we all get ourselves up to bed early, eh, girls? And speaking of days, don't forget, tomorrow's a shiny new one!"

It doesn't take long for everyone to disappear. Lulu, Toshio and Zed go off to their ground-floor rooms, with Twinkle tip-tapping after Zed, since she sleeps in a snuffly pile next to his bed.

Mademoiselle Fabienne and Miss Amethyst tipetty-tap up to their no-doubt fragrant rooms at the top of the house, as all of us St Grizzle girls go to our respective dorms on the first floor.

While Swan glides off to brush her teeth, I head to Fungi dorm, where I wriggle into my PJs and sigh. My sighs are for a jumble of reasons...

• happy sighs, cos no one is cross with me being in charge of the filming any more

• glum sighs, cos I have NO fab ideas for the filming, and

• confused sighs, cos I somehow got my head stuck inside the PJ top for a minute there.

"Well, whoo for me – my plan worked," says Swan coming into the dorm *just* as I wriggle my head free. "You're back in control, Dani!"

"Yeah, but back in control of what?" I reply as I lean on the windowsill and stare out at the dark woods beyond the garden. "Tomorrow's Tuesday already, which doesn't exactly give us much time to come up with something."

"Didn't you listen to my mum? Tomorrow's a shiny new day," Swan says with an unbothered yawn. "We'll figure something out. Night!"

"Night," I reply.

As Swan pings out the dorm light, I watch the stars outside ping on.

I suddenly wish I could speak to Granny Viv... In the excitement of the evening, I hadn't tried to call her and she was obviously too busy with her broken-down Mini woes to get back to me.

But I bet Granny Viv would know what to do for the film project – she's full of excellent ideas. Once, she offered herself when I was stuck for a show-and-tell idea at school. Everyone was well impressed that a gran could still do the splits. And when I didn't have a clue what to wear to Polly Brown's fancy-dress party, Granny Viv went and bought me a giant rubber ring, superglued some marshmallows to it and turned me into a Krispy Kreme doughnut. I won second prize.

I sigh (again) as another wibbly wiggle of homesickness hits me.

Off in the distance, a faraway dog **"ARF! ARF! ARF!"**s and I *almost* imagine it's Downboy...

Chapter 6

If You Go Down to the Woods Today...

And a sort-of treasure map...

"Due to unforeseen circumstances, our school timetable this week will be 'fluid'," Lulu announced at breakfast the next day.

I wasn't totally sure what that meant, apart from "wet", so I had to check with Swan.

"Lulu's trying to say that we won't stick *exactly* to the usual classes," she'd explained. "I bet we'll be doing more 'Life Skills' lessons than usual!"

Only I didn't totally get that either.

"I mean, we're all going to do more housework and cooking, till Lulu finds a new Mrs Hedges," Swan spelt out.

So today, Tuesday, is a big laundry day. The Newts have been given the job of stripping all the beds, though when I passed their dorm five minutes ago, that seemed to consist of them getting inside the empty duvets covers and squidging around on the floor, pretending to be slugs.

Downstairs in the utility room off the kitchen, the triplets are sorting out the washing into "whites", "coloureds" and "darks", which is taking ages – they're holding up one T-shirt/pillowcase/sock at a time and then having an intense, whispered conversation about it till they make up their minds which of the three piles to put it in. This might take till *next* Tuesday to finish.

Presuming the triplets get a move on, it'll then be the Conkers' turn to take over once the wash has finished. They'll hang everything out, since they're tall enough to reach the washing line without standing on a box.

Once school's officially over, Miss Amethyst and Mademoiselle Fabienne are going to do the ironing – I heard them earlier discussing playlists and biscuit choices for the task ahead.

Lastly me, Swan and Zed will put the laundry

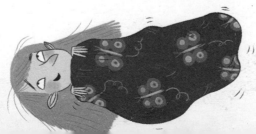

away before tea and make all the beds. It's our job to do that since we're the oldest and have more patience than the younger ones. They'll be bored of this particular "Life Skill" lesson by then and want to practise dance moves they saw on YouTube (Conkers), braid each other's hair in new and inventive ways (Otters) and scamper off to the tree house in the clearing in the woods to play Alien Vampire Cavemen or something (Newts).

But for now, with our current "fluid" timetable, we three Fungi have been allowed time out to investigate locations for the Why We Love Where We Live project.

Me and Swan are standing by the tree house and campfire pit, just about to set off into the woods. Zed is here, too, but he won't be coming with us cos the knobbly-bobbly tree roots in the woods make trekking in a wheelchair kind of tricky. (Boo.)

He's still been very helpful, though, and has

1) come up with a cool suggestion and

2) drawn us a map to find it.

"Look – there it is!" Zed announces, pointing at a scribbled-on piece of paper he's holding up to me and Swan. "See?"

"Oo-arrr!" I growl, doing my best pirate impersonation and making Swan snort.

I can't help it – Zed's just handed us something that looks like a *treasure* map, complete with dotted lines and an X marks the spot.

Only we're not hunting for treasure ... we're looking for a fairy ring.

Or at least what's *called* a fairy ring. When I was teeny, I always imagined it to be just like it sounded – a gathering of dinky fairies, skipping and **whee!**-ing in a circle. I remember being totally disappointed when someone told me it was just a bunch of mushrooms, which sit there in a ring not even dancing a little bit.

But now I'm older, and it sounds like it might be quite a special phenomenon. Also, I'm desperate.

Anyway, lying in bed last night, Zed remembered that Maryam and Maisie – two ex-pupils from when St Grizzle's was all straw hats and strict uniform – once came back to the school saying they'd found a perfect fairy ring, and described to him where it was.

"Will you take a photo to show me?" he asks me and Swan.

"Definitely, promise," I say, patting my hoodie pocket where my phone is.

"Yeah, and we'll take a picture of the treasure chest and all the swag, too," Swan adds to my pirate joke, as she snatches up the map.

"Very funny," Zed says wryly.

"Thank you, I know I am," says Swan and starts padding off through the undergrowth, with a quick order to Twinkle shouted over her shoulder.

"Oi, heel!"

Twinkle has been at the top of the ramp leading up to the tree house (which we built for Zed), happily headbutting the door. I don't know what's got her so excited – there's only some cushions and a spider or three in there.

It takes another, LOUDER "Oi, heel!" before she finally trip-traps down the ramp and skips over to join us.

"So, I reckon we'll need about five locations," I say as we follow the route Zed sketched and head north-east-ish, which should bring us to a foresters' track in a bit. Once we get there, we'll check the map again.

"Well, yeah, if that's how many Spencer and *his* lot are doing, we need to do the same," says Swan, before blowing a pink bubble. "Though maybe we should do MORE than them!"

"But we haven't even definitely got one yet," I remind her, before competitiveness blanks out her common sense. "We don't know if the mushrooms will still be th—"

Ding-a-ling-a-ling!

My mobile trills into life and, after a quick scrabble, I grab it out of my pocket and see that Granny Viv is calling.

"Hello, Dani, darling!" she says. "How's my favourite grandaughter?"

"Hi, Granny Viv!" I say, beaming. "It's so nice to hear your voice properly."

"And it's so nice to hear yours! Ooh, I feel like scooping you up and giving you a great big hug right now..."

I grin, and feel all warm and fuzzy inside.

"Well, that would be lovely but it's kind of impossible," I say, "since you're at home and I'm all the way away at St Grizzle's."

"Hmm... Yes, I suppose you're right," muttered Granny Viv, sounding disappointed. "Anyway, sorry it's taken an age to get back to you. Everything got complicated last night. I was having these endless ping-pong phone conversations with Eric."

Eric is a very good friend of Granny Viv's and

an old punk. When he's not being an antique punk and gigging, singing shouty songs, he fixes cars.

"Did he sort your engine?" I ask.

"No ... he wasn't around, darling. But he kept suggesting things for me to try. Sadly none of them worked, including begging the engine to start, pretty please!"

I smile, happy to hear Granny Viv joking around.

"But what are you up to, sweetheart?" she asks me.

"Well, I *should* be in normal lessons but the classes have all got changed around cos of a project," I say, then frown as something occurs to me. "So what are you doing phoning me now?"

"Ah … let's call it a grandmother's intuition," she says after a pause, which translates as "Oops, I didn't notice the time". "What ARE you doing, if you're not in normal lessons, then?"

"Me and Swan are in the woods that back on to the school grounds," I tell her as I watch Twinkle's white bum and twitchy tail bob ahead of us. "Our project is to make a film about where we live so we're having a mooch around to see if we can find something interesting."

"Ooh, lovely! Woods are magical places," Granny Viv enthuses. "I'm sure you'll find some gorgeous spots, like rocky outcrops and little waterfalls, and old carvings people did in tree bark years ago and maybe a fairy ring, since … well, since they *often* grow on forest floors."

"Wow! A fairy ring is *exactly* what we're looking for!" I say excitedly. "We heard that there's one somewhere near—"

"Dani! C'mere!" Swan calls out.

She's hurried ahead after Twinkle and it looks as if she's found something. Is it the fairy ring already? But we haven't come across the foresters' track yet... Unless we didn't figure out the map properly and have come a different way.

I'd better catch Swan up. It would be a disaster if the fairy ring is amazing and then Twinkle eats it before we get a chance to film anything.

"What's your friend shouting?" asks Granny Viv.

"She's just calling for me," I say, my voice going juddery as I start bobbing under branches and weaving over roots. "I think she might have found the fairy ring."

"I'd better let you go then," I hear Granny Viv say wistfully. "Will you call me later and let me know how you're getting on, Dani? It all sounds very exciting."

"Sure – I'll ping you a photo if we find anything cool," I hurriedly promise her. "Bye!"

I catch sight of Swan's sheeny-shiny long hair just up ahead and hurry towards her with a big ball of giddy in my chest.

Till she turns round and I see that *she's* not looking exactly giddy, and has her finger held to her lips.

"What is it?" I hiss as I catch her up.

Swan says nothing but just points.

There, up ahead, is the foresters' track – and parked across it is a beat-up old camper van.

"So? What about it?" I say, talking louder. It's not as if we're looking at something sinister, like a WWII tank or a spy's car with blacked-out windows or a vintage hearse or something. If camper vans could look friendly, then this one does. It's got flower stickers around the headlights and is painted purple.

"What's it doing here?" Swan insists on whispering as we take a few, tentative steps forward.

"Maybe the driver's taking their dog for a walk in the forest?" I suggest, since people do like walking in forests, particularly with their dogs. It's not exactly rocket science.

"Yeah, and the driver's making themselves totally at home. Look – there's washing hanging up!"

OK, now that IS a bit odd, I think, looking at the towel and jeans dangling between two nearby trees.

"They've even got a camping stove," hisses Swan.

I glance at the ground and, sure enough, there's a camping stove by the door of the camper van, complete with a small silver pot containing what looks like baked beans. A plate's been left beside it, which Twinkle is licking so hard she's pushing it under the van.

"And they must've been here like, *really* recently," hisses Swan.

"How can you be so sure, Detective Swan?" I lightheartedly ask my friend.

"There's still steam coming out of the pot on the stove."

I study the wisps of hot air rising for about half a second and then all the hairs rise up on my arms.

It's like me and Swan (and Twinkle) are Goldilocks(es) and three camper-van-driving bears are about to crash through the trees and come after us at any second.

I turn to look at Swan and she turns to look at me.

We have the same word on the tip of our tongues, I'm sure, and it's not porridge.

"RUN!"

Chapter 7

Imprisoned by Hyper Newts

And a surprise
visitor...

We don't stop till we flop breathless on the back lawn, hearts pounding.

Lulu is there and frowns at me and Swan, wondering what's going on.

But she finds it impossible to ask us, since a cluster of eight-year-olds are bouncing around her like Tiggers, jabbering at loud volume.

Lulu is trying desperately to calm and shush them but they have tipped over the edge of reason and there doesn't seem to be any way to haul them back to normality, apart from chucking a bucket of cold water over them.

I spot concerned faces at the windows –
Conkers, Otters, Zed and the teachers, all
wondering what on earth is going on.

"Girls! QUIETEN DOWN!" Lulu roars, to
absolutely no effect.

And then I notice Toshio ambling out of the
back door, his headphones round his neck, the
ever-present polite smile on his face.

In his hand is a megaphone. As he gets closer
to the mayhem, he raises it to his mouth.

**"SHUT UP NOW, PLEASE! AND
THANK YOU VERY MUCH!"**

It does the trick. The Newts are so stunned by Toshio's blaring voice that they freeze – and look at the megaphone longingly. I hope Toshio goes back into the office and locks it up somewhere they can't get a hold of it, or life – with amplified Newts – could become unbearable.

"Excellent, Toshio," says Lulu. "I really appreciate your ingenuity."

Toshio smiles and nods. I don't think he understood a word Lulu said, apart from "Toshio", but he can certainly tell that...

1) Lulu is pleased, and

2) what he did worked.

"Right!" Lulu says, addressing the Newts again, now they've stopped going off like fireworks. "Can just one of you tell me what's wrong? Blossom?"

I swap glances with Swan. What's going on around here? *We've* both been spooked by someone living in the woods, and now the *Newts* have been spooked by something, too.

Is it the same thing?

The same someone?

"Lulu!" screeches Blossom, bouncing so much that the small twigs that seem permanently lodged in her hair fall right out. "There is a

WITCH LIVING IN OUR TREE HOUSE!"

Me and Swan glance at each other and our shoulders sink in unison.

We are NOT thinking about the same thing.

The Newts are lovely but they are lovely twits, and have just dreamed up something ridiculous.

Actually, maybe me and Swan sort of dreamed up something ridiculous, too. Why did we panic so much at the sight of an empty pot of beans and a towel left out to dry?

"There's a witch living in the tree house?" says Lulu, raising her eyebrows. "Well, she has VERY good taste. It's an extremely well-built and good-looking tree house."

She glances over at us, still flumped on the grass. She's looking at Swan in particular, cos it was Swan who spray-painted the most amazing black crow in flight on the front of the tree house.

Though I think Lulu is also glancing over to check we're OK and letting us know that she'll come to us asap after she's dealt with the ... er ... "witch" issue.

"So, Blossom, what did this witch person look like?" asks Lulu.

Behind her, Zed is rolling his way out of the back door of the house, followed by a raggle-taggle bunch of curious Conkers and Otters plus Miss Amethyst and Mademoiselle Fabienne.

It's at that moment that I realize ONE important person isn't there. By that I mean, one important goat.

"Twinkle!" I hiss at Swan and her almond eyes widen.

We ran and ran and RAN out of the woods, without remembering that we'd left Twinkle behind. Zed's going to KILL us!

"We saw the witch looking out of the tree-house window!" I vaguely hear Blossom say in my panic. "She had a **CLAW** around something and this **BRIGHT RED** hair and she was making this awful sort of **'ARF! ARF! ARF!'** sound!"

A thought tries to wriggle and squiggle to the front of my frazzled mind. But just before it does, I hear a familiar voice.

"Um, excuse me? I think I'M your witch..."

I flip my head round and there's Granny Viv, walking out of the woods in all her mad, red-haired glory. She smiles apologetically as she lifts the thermos mug in her "claw".

Trotting happily by her side is Twinkle.

I'm just about to squawk, "What on EARTH are you DOING here?" when a big blur of fur and drool hurtles towards me at high speed.

OOF!

Two huge paws pin my shoulders to the ground and my face is covered in frantic shlurps.

Well, hello to you, too, Downboy!

Chapter 8

Room for a Little One?

And the guided tour...

"Ooh, this is nice, isn't it?" says Granny Viv, sinking into the beanbag next to mine in Lulu's office.

As Granny Viv stares admiringly at Swan's artwork on the walls, I stare at her, not quite believing she's actually here.

I'd have found out quicker, of course, if I'd paid attention to Twinkle.

Like a goat-shaped sniffer dog, she'd worked out that there was more than just some cushions and a bunch of spiders in the tree house and that's why she'd been headbutting the door earlier.

Meanwhile, me, Swan and Zed were down at the campfire pit, goofing around about treasure maps, without realizing that BEHIND the thunked door lurked a spying gran with, as it turns out...

• a restrained pooch
• a thermos of tea

- a stash of snacks (for humans AND doggies)
- a pair of binoculars.

Back out on the lawn, Granny Viv said she'd had to hold on to Downboy's snout very hard to stop him **"ARF! ARF! ARF!"**ing at the goat on the other side of the door and that he'd wriggled and squiggled like MAD when he'd heard my voice.

She tried to say some other stuff about what on earth she was doing in the tree house but it got jumbled up and lost in the confusion of happily hysterical Newts, dogs and goats.

That's why Lulu shooed me and Granny Viv into her office, so we could have a proper chat in peace.

"Here you are!" says Lulu, breezing into the room and handing Granny Viv a cup of tea.

"Thank you! Is Downboy all right out there?" Granny Viv checks.

"Seems to be," says Lulu, peering out of the window before she sits at her desk. "He's having a lovely time being chased around the garden by Twinkle. They're best of friends already. But, Viv, DO tell all! How long have you been spying on us?"

Lulu's eyes are sparkling at the notion of Granny Viv living "wild" in the woods.

She threw her head back and laughed when Granny Viv said she'd used the tree house as a secret, biscuit-eating den where she could nosey at the school and check on me without being seen. (It's a relief that Lulu thinks of Granny Viv's antics more as an adventure and less like an issue that should involve calling the police.)

"Well, I didn't *set out* to spy on you. It was all a bit of a whim, really, starting with the camper van," Granny Viv says brightly. "I saw it in the local garage last weekend, with a 'For Sale' sign and thought what fun it would be to buy it. I imagined coming down here to take Dani away for the weekend now and again. Whisking her off for Granny and Grandaughter escapades!"

Lulu raises her eyebrows as if that does indeed sound like such fun.

"OK," I say from the squidging comfort of the other beanbag, "you swapped your Mini for a camper van. But what's that got to do with you hiding away in the tree house?"

"Hiding? Oh, that makes me sound like I ran away from home, doesn't it? A runaway granny. Ha!" Granny Viv says, grinning. "But honestly, darling, it was all a bit of an accident. You see, once I bought Daisy—"

"Daisy?" I interrupt.

"—the camper van, darling, her name's Daisy," Granny Viv breezes on. "As soon as I bought Daisy, I decided I'd take her for a spin, pack some picnic things and make a day of it with Downboy. And then I thought, what if I drive in the direction of Dani's new school? What if I park nearby and then have a sneaky peek, just to make sure she's OK?"

"So you got here this morning?" I ask, though I'm trying to work out why Granny Viv had washing hanging from tree branches if she'd only arrived shortly before me and Swan discovered her van on the foresters' track.

"Oh, no! I was out for a Sunday drive!" laughs Granny Viv. "But then I got completely lost down these tracks in the woods and it was getting later and later. I parked up and was trying to figure out where I was – but when I tried to start Daisy up again, her engine clapped out. So Downboy and I ended up sleeping there all night – the benches in the back convert into comfy beds and there's the sweetest little checked curtains! We were ever so snug in there."

Granny Viv's explanation is gently wandering off-course, and I'm worried it might get as lost as *she* was.

"Sunday? But it's Tuesday now," I point out. "What have you been doing all this time?"

"Well, I suppose I've been trying to contact

Eric, trying to start the engine and trying to catch sight of you, sweetie," Granny Viv answers, as if all of that is pretty straightforward and normal. Which it is, if you live in **CRAZYVILLE**.

"You got a *really* close sighting of me this morning," I say with a little frown. "I mean, I was right below the tree house. Why didn't you just come out and say hello?"

"Oh, Dani, darling... I so wanted to but I thought you might be cross with me," Granny Viv replies, squishing round in her beanbag to look at me better. "You know, silly, old grandmother, embarrassing you in front of your new friends! So I just phoned you instead, once you'd walked away into the trees."

Ah, that conversation when I was hurrying after Swan and Twinkle. No wonder Granny

Viv had such excellent suggestions about what "magical" locations we might find in the woods. She wasn't just *imagining* that there'd be carvings in trees and fairy rings and the rest – she'd actually found them!

"And I thought if Eric could help me get Daisy up and running, I'd be gone before anyone knew I'd been here – especially you, Dani!" Granny Viv adds with a shrug. "That's till I managed to frighten all those sweet little girls. I'm so sorry about that, Lulu!"

"Oh, don't worry about the Newts – they're a hardy bunch," says Lulu, with a wave of her hand. "But anyway, who's Eric?"

"He's my friend – and car mechanic," Granny Viv explains. "He's away this week but he's been trying to give me tips over the phone to get Daisy going. None of them worked, unfortunately."

"Oh dear," Lulu murmurs sympathetically.

"So what do you..."

As Lulu and Granny Viv chat about broken-down camper van issues, I tune out, and suddenly start to make sense of the two snatched conversations I've had with Granny Viv the last couple of mornings...

• yesterday, she'd sounded kerfuffled when I mentioned her Mini but of course, unknown to me, she'd traded it in for Daisy

• today, she'd asked why I wasn't in normal lessons. That wasn't down to "grandmother's intuition" like she said – it was cos she was watching us from the tree house!

And then I suddenly have the funniest feeling I'm being stared at.

Possibly because Lulu and Granny Viv are both staring at me.

"What do you think?" Granny Viv asks me.

It's obviously something I should be pleased

about or she wouldn't be grinning like the Cheshire Cat.

"Would you like it if your grandmother stayed for a few days?" Lulu spells things out more clearly. "Till her friend can get here at the weekend and fix the camper van?"

I am so, so, SO pleased I go to throw my arms around Granny Viv.

But because leaping out of a beanbag is impossible, it turns into a sort of half-hearted *lunge* with arms flailing.

Still, Granny Viv understands and, anyway, she's having the same problem as me.

So instead, she blows me a red-lipped ***mwah*** of a kiss and it feels almost as good as any hug.

Could this day get any better?

"Fantastic!" says Lulu, slapping her hands on the desk. "Well, you know how the old saying goes

– there's always room for a little one! How about you get your gran settled in one of the spare rooms on the third floor, Dani? There're lots to choose from. Then maybe Viv could sit in on some of your lessons and get a feel for what goes on here at St Grizzle's!"

What goes on at St Grizzle's? A whole lot of bonkers.

So Granny Viv should fit right in...

"...and I just LOVE the colour of Miss Amethyst's hair!" says Granny Viv as we walk along the village high street with Downboy and Twinkle.

I *knew* Granny Viv would adore Miss Amethyst's powder puff of mauve hair. Just like I knew she'd adore Miss Amethyst. She sat knitting a multi-coloured scarf at the back of Miss Amethyst's science lesson earlier this morning but soon threw her knitting needles aside and had her hand up in the air, desperate to answer questions along with the rest of us.

And in our art lesson, Granny Viv ended up drumming the desk softly in time to the prettily sad strumming of Mademoiselle Fabienne's guitar. Then she got as excited as everyone else about making a papier-mâché model. Granny Viv's is of Daisy the camper van and is really quite good. Mine is of Downboy but looks more like a potato cow.

"But anyway, enough about the school. Tell me more about this fantastic-sounding film project," Granny Viv says. "Your mother will be so proud when she hears you're the director!"

With her full-on schedule in the freezing Antarctic, I don't know when I'll next get a chance to talk to Mum. I sent her a link to the rolling-green-hills film with its grazing potato-cows and giant-mutant-goat but I don't think she's seen it yet (at least she hasn't given me a "Like" yet).

"Don't get *too* excited," I tell Granny Viv. "It's not for Hollywood – just for the local council's new website."

"Well, it's all good experience for you, Dani," my grandmother says matter-of-factly. "But what are you looking so down about? You usually love making mini-movies."

"I do ... it's just the deadline is teatime tomorrow. We've seen some pretty spots in the woods but we haven't finally settled on any locations yet," I explain, "let alone started filming."

"Hmm. Whatever you do, please don't use *that* monstrosity," says Granny Viv, pointing to the ugly car park opposite the supermarket. "I mean, was the architect who built that blindfolded when they designed it? Or did they just get a kick out of making people grumpy?"

Once Granny Viv heard about our lack of dinner lady – and food in general – she offered to make a giant vat of veggie chilli for everyone's lunch and that's why we're here, hunting and gathering kidney beans. It's the least she could do to repay Lulu's hospitality, she says.

I think Lulu thought it would be nice to let me and Granny Viv catch up, too.

And so far on the way here, I've pointed out St Grizzle (wearing striped oven gloves today), told Granny Viv what happened with Mrs Hedges (i.e. that she didn't enjoy her ghostly makeover) and explained to her why the Newts have been a bit funny towards her so far this morning (they're disappointed she wasn't *really* a witch).

And now that Granny Viv's got a bit of background on the school and everyone in it, it's nice to show her the village, cos Huddleton is very pretty, apart from the parts that aren't.

"It's as if architects build new stuff without looking at what's already there," I say, gazing around at the cute old buildings that line most of the street.

"True, true... Like a zookeeper sticking a buffalo in the otter enclosure and thinking it's a close enough match," Granny Viv muses. "Can you picture how the village would've looked when St Grizelda's School for Girls was first built, Dani? Can you imagine the first ever head teacher strolling along here with her pupils fanning out behind her?"

Granny Viv stands straight, nose in the air, imitating some grand and strict head teacher from a hundred years or so ago. Though the only thing we have fanning behind us is a shopping trolley, a goat and a tongue-lolling dog. (After a few experimental headbutts, Twinkle decided Downboy was OK and now they're trotting along like a pair of small, freaky-looking ponies.)

"What would Miss— what did you say her name was again?" Granny asks, continuing with her funny, proud-peacock strutting.

"Miss Augusta Wilberbuttle," I tell her, remembering what Yas had said during the Conkers' attempt at a film.

"Ah, yes! Now what do you suppose the fine, upstanding Miss Augusta Wilberbuttle would make of some of these clunky modern horrors?"

I'm just about to answer Granny Viv when we hear a shout.

"Ooh, hold your nose, guys – it's some smelly Grizzlers! Ha ha ha!"

Uh-oh.

"Grizzlers..." repeats Granny Viv, her ears pricking up. "Do they mean St Grizzle's?"

"Yep," I reply. "Anyway, here's the supermarket."

It's time to get on with the shopping and away from the teasing. But first we need to tie Twinkle and Downboy to the nearest lamppost.

"Oi! OI!" comes a shout, from a shouter who clearly wants our attention "SHE'S a bit old to be a Grizzler, isn't she?"

There's only one person who'd have the nerve to be that cheeky about a grown-up.

"Friend of yours?" asks Granny Viv, looking across the road at Spencer and his gaggle of sniggering mates.

Spencer's holding a camera in his hand – the school's new bit of kit that he was boasting about yesterday.

"Couldn't be *less* of a friend," I tell her, though Granny Viv is obviously smart enough to know an idiot when she sees one. "Spencer goes to the local village school. He likes to act as if his school and St Grizzle's are big rivals, even though we couldn't care less."

"Wait a minute – is it that SWAN girl, with a new look?" Spencer carries on, not knowing when to stop. "Red hair and wrinkles ... interesting way to go. Ha ha ha ha!"

"Wow, he really is quite something," mutters Granny Viv, as if that something is the sort of something you might find stuck on your shoe if you're very unlucky.

"They're entering the council's competition, too," I tell her. "He told me and Swan yesterday that *they've* claimed all the best locations around here and that we can't use them in our film."

"Best locations like what?" asks Granny Viv, bending to tie Downboy's lead to the lamppost, while I do the same with Twinkle's.

"Like the war memorial over there and the bridge down the side street here and the market cross and the pretty old church and the duck pond on the green at the other end of the road..."

"Hmm," Granny Viv murmurs thoughtfully but I have no idea what those thoughts might be.

"So, shall we ignore them? Shall we get our shopping?" I suggest, turning my back on the still-sniggering Spencer and co.

"Absolutely!" Granny Viv says cheerfully – then hands me the shopping list. "You start without me, Dani. I just want to have a quick look around the village and then join you. Won't be long! All right?"

Saying no to Granny Viv is virtually impossible. Mind you, she's usually saying stuff like, "Shall we eat ALL the cake, Dani?" or "Let's do roly-polys down the hill and see who gets there first!"

So this time I'm kind of confused. Doing shopping on my own while she sightsees doesn't sound a whole lot of fun.

I'd quite like to say, "No, it's not all right."

But instead, I mumble a disappointed and useless "Mneh..." as Granny Viv strides off.

If she's been so keen to see me all this time, why is she so keen to get away from me all of a sudden...?

Chapter 9
Crocheting Spaghetti... Near Enough

And a sea of socks...

Help!

I have gone past the point of no return.

I have entered the danger zone.

I have ignored the sign at the door that reads:

Newts burrow here.
Death to Introoders!!

And the reason I have dared to risk the wrath of the Newts?

Well, it's because I need to put their clean bedding on, since that was the deal with the laundry today.

Zed is ferrying all the sheets and duvet sets to the bottom of the stairs, and me and Swan are gathering them up and getting busy up on the

first floor. We tossed a coin and I lost – she's
doing the Conkers, Otters and Fungi dorms (nine
beds) and I'm doing the Newts (ten beds).

"Urgh ... gross," says Arch as I hold my phone
up and scan the room so my friend back home
can see how incredibly brave I am.

It is very gross.

Every Newt has scrawled a self-portrait of
themselves on the wall behind their beds and
every one of them looks like a version of some
evil Halloween pumpkin-head.

And then there's the socks. So many socks.
Floppy, worn socks ALL over the floor of the
dorm. How can ten girls have THAT many socks?
Is it even possible, or allowed?

"Just be glad you can only see and not smell,"
I tell Arch as I prop him up on the nearest bedside
cabinet, so he can keep me company while I
wrestle with duvet covers.

It's so good to catch up with Arch at last, even if I am stuck in Smelly-Sock Land. I've just filled him in on all the dramas of the last couple of days and he's found it highly entertaining, especially since the only drama he's had was at lunchtime today, when the dinner hut ran out of sticky toffee pudding. (Noooo!)

"Hold on..." says Arch, disappearing from view

for a minute or two, though I can hear some banging and clattering in the background.

And then a face – sort of – appears on the small screen again.

OK, so it's a hand puppet made out of a sock, with two googly eyes stuck on.

"So, Dani," says a high-pitched voice as the sock puppet mimes the words, "is it totally great

having your granny and your dog with you
right now?"

"Very funny," I say in a sarcastic way, though
the sock thing IS pretty funny, considering. "And
yes and no."

"Yes and no what?" says Arch, his face
coming back into view, even though he's still
got the sock puppet doing the "voice".

"I mean, yes, it's completely brilliant
having Granny Viv and Downboy here,"
I answer him.

"But?" says the sock-puppet Arch.

"But what?" I ask as I carry on putting pillows
into pillowcases and duvets into duvet covers.
"I didn't say but."

"Dani, you just PUNCHED that pillow into its
case," the sock puppet/Arch points out. "So there
has to be a but."

"Well, I s'pose," I say with a sigh.

I mean, there was that whole thing at the supermarket where Granny Viv left me to do the shopping on my own for HALF AN HOUR (I had to wait outside with the packed shopping trolley and two restless animals for ages). Then Granny Viv was all weird and vague and fake cheerful and wouldn't tell me what she'd been doing while she'd been gone.

"Spill," the sock puppet/Arch orders.

"OK..." I mumble. "It's just that I've hardly seen either of them since lunch. Downboy's been off scampering with Twinkle and Granny Viv didn't come to afternoon classes."

"Well, she IS sixty-five and doesn't technically have to go to school any more," says Arch, forgetting about the sock on his hand and letting it flop sideways like it's fainted.

"I know," I reply, shrugging. "But she's made herself totally at home already. She sat gossiping with Miss Amethyst at lunchtime. And the Newts forgave her for not being a witch and sang her a hello song they just made up on the spot."

"Did it have a tune?" asks Arch.

"No, but that's not the point. And the triplets ALMOST smiled at her, Arch! It's freaky how well she's getting on with everyone. AND Lulu let Granny Viv sit in her office all afternoon while she was teaching and I don't know what she's been doing in there..."

OK, so I'm sounding all moany and whiny.

And I know I'm not just moany and whiny about how quickly Granny Viv's settled in.

"Anyway, what ARE you going to do for the film project, Dani?" says Arch, since it's mainly what I phoned him to talk about.

"Haven't a clue..." I sigh, punching another pillow into its cover.

Honestly, if there was a Society for the Prevention of Cruelty to Pillows, I would be in pretty serious trouble right now.

"Hey, you know, *maybe*," says Arch, the peak of his red baseball cap bobbing as he talks on my phone screen, "you could still film at the same spots as Spencer and his mates. Why should THEY claim all the best stuff in the village?"

"I just don't fancy copying what they're doing," I tell him, "especially if they're filming on a fancy, professional camera."

"Yeah, but you could make it different, Dani," says Arch. "How about you edit YOUR film with a weird filter, like distorting stuff with a fish-eye lens, or use freaky colours, or have it spinning like a kaleidoscope or something?"

"Suppose that could look cool but too much weirdness might frighten visitors away, rather than attract them?" I suggest, though I don't want to dampen Arch's enthusiasm.

"OK, fair enough," he says. "Well, how about you shoot all the scenes with the T rex as your presenter? You could have it moving around a bit as it talks, with you adding a funny voiceover after!"

"Hmm. But having a random Tyrannosaurus rex narrate a promotional film about the beauty of the area around St Grizzle's ... it sounds kind of, well, maybe a teeny bit *random*?"

Urgh. I'd hoped Arch would magically say something that would solve my project problem but I'm no closer to finding a filming solution. And it's Tuesday teatime already! Earlier, I heard Lulu tell Granny Viv that she has no idea how she'll get the whole of St Grizzle's to the awards ceremony all the way away in Dunchester on Friday, cos the minibus is too tiddly. I'm secretly hoping Lulu decides it's too much trouble to go, cos we haven't got a film – or the faintest inkling of an idea about what to film – to even enter the competition!

KNOCKITTY-KNOCK-KNOCK!

"Hello, sweetheart!" Granny Viv says as she wanders into the dorm, then pulls a face. "Ooh, interesting décor in here…"

"You could always ask the Newts to style *your* room," I cheekily suggest, thinking of the flowery-wallpapered bedroom Granny Viv's staying in.

"Hmm, tempting, but I don't think I'm brave enough for this much mess," Granny Viv replies as she kicks some socks away. "Anyway, can I give you a hand, Dani?"

"Um, yes, please," I say gratefully, since putting a duvet cover on to a duvet is about as simple as crocheting with spaghetti.

"Great!" says Granny Viv, getting on with the duvet fitting/spaghetti crocheting as if it's all ridiculously easy-peasy. "Actually, I'm glad I've got you all to myself, Dani."

I'm about to point out that we're not totally alone, since Arch and his sock buddy are perched on the nearest bedside table, but Granny Viv breezes on with what she has to say.

"Want to know what I found out?"

"Mum's at the wrong Pole?" I suggest. "All the penguins moved to the Arctic instead, just to mess with the scientists?"

"Well, I wouldn't put it past them. Sneaky lot, penguins, behind all that cuteness," says Granny Viv, nodding as if I have a fair point. "But want to know what I REALLY found out?"

"OK," I say, hoping she means that a gold ticket she's found in a bar of chocolate will give us a year's free supply of the stuff.

Or a raffle ticket in an old coat pocket has won us an hour in a room filled with puppies.

Or that she's discovered a secret portal in time and space at the back of her camper van that'll take me to the Antarctic, so I can give my mum a quick hug.

ANY of those would be nice.

"Well, I have found out a couple of things, actually," says Granny Viv, with a big wanna-know-my-secrets grin. "Did I ever tell you that I was the tour manager for Eric's punk band in the summer of 1977?"

"Er, no..." I reply, wondering where on earth this is going.

"Well, I was, and that meant me being in charge of these loud and lazy blokes and driving them and their gear all over Europe in a beat-up old van. Can you imagine?"

"Sort of," I say, thinking nothing Granny Viv does would surprise me. "Um, but what's this got to do with finding things out?"

"Ah, well, I was on Lulu's computer earlier, looking up recipes and dreaming up meals for the rest of this week, just to help her out. And while I was online, I decided to check something on my driving licence..."

So *that's* what Granny Viv was up to. The thing is, the meal-planning I get, but why have driving licence checks got her all excited?

"...and I found out that I'm also allowed to drive coaches."

"So...?" I say hesitantly.

"So I booked one – and I'm driving us all to the awards ceremony at Dunchester Town Hall on Friday!"

"What? But we haven't even got a film to enter!" I protest, feeling wibbly around the edges.

"Not a problem," says Granny Viv, expertly tossing a duvet into its cover like she's flipping a pancake. "Cos the SECOND thing I found out was that Miss Amethyst used to be an actress. She was in panto and everything!"

It's as if Granny Viv is talking in riddles. One second she's on about recipes, the next coach companies and now it's Miss Amethyst's former

career on the stage. The madness of the Newts'
dorm was already making my head feel fuzzy but
Granny Viv is making my mind melt.

"Um … yeah, I know that she used to be an
actress. I mean, Miss Amethyst is our drama
teacher, after all," I say, frowning, and wondering
where this conversation's going next.

"I thought she was your science teacher?"
Granny Viv frowns back, not realizing quite
HOW much everyone has to do at St Grizzle's.
"Oh, never mind, that's not the point. Finding that
out about Miss Amethyst – PLUS something you
and I spoke about today, Dani – has given me an
amazing idea for your Why We Love Where We
Live project. Want to hear it?"

You know something? Part of me wants to say
no. Cos part of me is feeling a teeny bit hugely
cross that Granny Viv has just waltzed in and
made herself quite comfy at St Grizzle's, all in

the blink of an eye.

St Grizzle's is MY school, not hers.

I'M the director of this film project, not Granny Viv.

It should be ME who—

"**YES!**" a tiny, tinny voice shouts from the bedside cabinet. "**I WANT TO HEAR IT!**"

Oops, I forgot about my miniaturized best friend for a minute there.

"Ha!" laughs Granny Viv, grabbing up my phone and my screen-sized buddy. "Isn't it all such good fun, Arch? Don't you just LOVE this place?"

"Mneh…" I mumble, and hide my grumpy face behind a fluffy duvet.

Three of my most favourite things in the world are Granny Viv, Arch and making mini-movies.

But right now, I wish … oh, I don't know what I wish.

"Hey," says Swan, appearing at the doorway of the dorm, twirling a stretchy twang of pink bubblegum around her finger.

"Hey," I say back, trying – and failing – to do a convincing smile.

"Hi, Swan! Have you met Arch?" booms Granny Viv, who's literally holding my best friend in the palm of her hand.

"We've said hello a couple of times," Swan replies, giving a swift chin nod to Arch.

"I was just about to tell these two my idea for the film," says Granny Viv, pointing at me and my phone.

"Yeah, so I heard," says Swan.

"Great! Well, come on in and sit down, and I'll tell you all about it at the same time..." says Granny Viv, parking herself on the newly made bed and patting the space beside her.

What, she wants to snaffle Swan, too?

"Uh, sure," Swan answers with a shrug. "But could I grab Dani for a few minutes first? I just need her to give me a hand with something."

"Of course!" Granny Viv says brightly and then carries on nattering with Arch.

Swan leaves at high-speed, and zips across the corridor to our dorm, with me trailing behind, dragging a half-made duvet in my clenched fist.

BANG! goes the dorm door.

"What do you need me to do?" I ask.

"Take THAT," Swan orders, pointing to the duvet, "hold it to your face and scream!"

"Huh?" I mumble.

"I heard your gran. I saw your face. My mum drives me mad when she takes over like that, too. So I thought I'd rescue you – let you have an **AAAAARGHHHH!** moment."

Ooh, you know I think that Swan might be *another* of my favourite things.

Cos if knowing when someone needs to go **AAAAARGHHHH!** isn't the sign of a good friend, then I don't know what is.

Chapter 10
Fingers-crossed-and-no-jinx

And feeling
invisible...

"Doesn't she look amazing?" says Granny Viv, stepping away from Miss Amethyst and revealing her "look" to everyone on Wednesday morning (i.e. the whole school, which happens to be crammed into Lulu's office).

"**Whoo-OOO-ooo!**" Miss Amethyst calls out, making all the Newts shriek and giggle.

So, what's going on? Well, Granny Viv – with the help of Mademoiselle Fabienne – has transformed Miss Amethyst into St Grizzle's first ever head teacher, Miss Augusta Wilberbuttle.

As a ghost.

Her make-up is white, her hair is white, her sweeping old-fashioned skirt and cape are white.

And the ghostly Miss Wilberbuttle is going to be the narrator of our Why We Love Where We Live film project. She is going to give her early 20th century opinion on the 21st century best and worst bits around St Grizzle's School and the village.

This was the idea Granny Viv explained to me, Swan and a tiny Arch-on-the-screen last night in the Newts dorm. It was inspired, she said, by stuff I'd told her about on our walk to Huddleton for the groceries, stuff like Mrs Hedges' ghostly sheet tangle and the impressive speech about Miss Wilberbuttle on the Conkers' mini-film.

At the time, we all thought it was pretty great. This morning, it's obvious everyone else thinks it's pretty great, too.

But still, Granny Viv and her Great Idea is

making me feel...

AAAAARGHHHH!

"Be cool," mutters Swan. She can sense the top of my head is about to pop off.

Here's the thing – back at home, everyone, and I mean **EVERYONE**, loves, and I mean LOVES, Granny Viv. All her friends, all her neighbours, all her workmates from before she retired, everyone of the 473 "friends" on her Facebook page loves, loves, loves Granny Viv.

And of course, I love her the most, cos she's my gran and everything, and she is totally the best.

And even though she's only been here for practically a nano-second, everyone at St Grizzle's seems to love Granny Viv, too, which is, er, lovely.

But that's the problem – everyone going wild for Granny Viv has happened TOO quickly and it's making me feel INVISIBLE. And don't even get me started on the fact that she has come up with her Great Idea for the film project when I couldn't.

And right this minute, with everyone from the smallest of the Newts to boss of the school Lulu staring at Granny Viv and hanging on her every word as if she's a genius, I feel like handing my phone right over to my grandmother and telling HER to film it all.

Maybe I can go hang out with Twinkle and Downboy and chew scattered pegs on the lawn instead...

"Well, that's all sounding fabulous! TOTALLY inspired!" says Lulu. "So, what happens next?"

"Well, we film 'Miss Wilberbuttle' beside some of the worst new buildings, giving her opinion of them," says Granny Viv, "and then we switch and take her to these beautiful hidden-away spots in the woods, and hear all the wonderful things she she has to say about them. It'll be a brilliant contrast."

"I can't wait!" says white-faced, white-lipped, utter-spooky Miss Amethyst. "Where's my script?"

"Script...?" Granny Viv says, sounding confused. "Can't you just make your speech up as you go along?"

"Improvise? Oh, no, darling, I'm not that sort of an actress," Miss Amethyst replies, a frown starting to crack her white facepaint. "I need to know my lines!"

Suddenly, I think of someone who loves Granny Viv as much as I do, but feels **AAAAARGHHHH!** about her quite a lot. I've never, ever understood why my quiet, sensible, organized mum gets so grouchy with Granny Viv but now I think I get it. Granny Viv is like a big showy Catherine wheel, spinning off in all directions and grabbing everyone's attention but with nothing much to add once the fizzles and flashes have died away. And maybe loud and sparkly Granny Viv makes Mum feel a little bit invisible, too.

I don't have much time to think about this, though – I'm distracted by a thumping noise. It's Zed... He's gently thudding the rubber tyre of his wheelchair up against Lulu's desk, while STARING at me. Is Zed trying to attract my attention? I frown at him, and wonder why he's pulling a funny face. He's either got a bad tummyache or is trying to tell me something.

Maybe I'm a bit thick but I don't get it.

Zed seems to *get* that I don't get it, so he says VERY loudly, "Hey, Dani – YOU'RE the director. What should we do?"

"WE" – that's the word that makes a switch flick on in my brain.

"Um…" I start with a mumble as everyone turns to look at me.

Deep breath, Dani, I tell myself, then try again.

"Thanks for coming up with this great idea, Granny Viv. But like Lulu told us at our assembly on Monday, this has to be a whole-school activity. So…"

I glance around at lots of expectant faces.

"I think Swan and Zed should have a production meeting with Granny Viv, to map out where all the pretty places in the woods are, and then we can plan our shooting schedule."

Granny Viv, Swan and Zed nod their okays, which makes me feel better and more in control.

"Yas? Can you write the script, please?"

Yas beams a *Yes, I can do this!*

"Angel, you could do the filming with Zed and help me with editing later. I'll teach you how the editing app works. And May-Belle, could you figure out some background music? Maybe moody goth stuff for the modern bits and nice jangly guitars for the scenes in the woods?"

Angel and May-Belle high-five each other.

"Otters and Newts... I need you to do some acting. Is that OK?"

Cue massive whoops from the Newts and strange smiles from the triplets. I hope they don't all get their hopes up and think that I mean they're going to have STARRING roles... I mostly just need them to goof around – being themselves – in the background.

One hand is up, though, which belongs to someone I haven't mentioned yet.

Klara is blinking at me hopefully with her white-fringed eyelashes.

"Yes, I think we'll definitely need some cartwheeling in the film," I tell her. Klara is so pleased she immediately rushes out of the office and does a bunch of practice cartwheels all down the corridor.

There actually appears to be a cartwheel going on in my tummy, too.

It's because I got brave and un-invisibled myself (don't care if that's not a real word), and came out from the shadow of Granny Viv. And I'm back to doing what I do best, i.e. making mini-movies but without Arch's help.

Only this mini-movie is bigger than anything I've done at home ... and I think maybe – fingers-crossed-and-no-jinx – everything will be all right!

Chapter 11
Bedazzled and Bewildered

And photobombing grans...

Dunchester Town Hall is like a giant school uniform warehouse.

Grey sweatshirts, turquoise sweatshirts, purple sweatshirts.

Navy blazers, black blazers, brown blazers.

Ties with blue stripes, red stripes, yellow stripes.

White shirts and coloured polo shirts.

School logos on every top and jacket.

And everywhere, everywhere, sheeny-shiny black shoes.

Then, filing in, there's **US**.

The only thing that's the same when it comes to we St Grizzle's girls (and our random boy) is that we don't match – at all.

Though it has to be said, we *are* wearing our cleanest T-shirts, jeans, shorts and leggings. To help out, Granny Viv stayed behind when we went filming in the village yesterday and did a

MASSIVE clothes wash. Turns out there actually IS a floor under the now-removed sock carpet in the Newts' dorm!

"OK, let's sit down and get settled, my lovelies!" Lulu says cheerfully, waving us into an empty row.

Quite a few kids from other schools snigger at that. But then I don't suppose those particular kids are the sort of pupils who teachers would ever refer to as "lovely". Swan narrows her eyes their way and blows then **POPs!** the biggest, most sarcastic bubble she can.

Other kids, who may well be lovely, turn to look at us the way a toddler might gawp longingly at someone holding an ice cream. You can tell from their expressions that they'd've *really* liked to wear a smiley T-shirt and flip-flops to today's ceremony, too, instead of a scratchy school jumper, a too-tight tie and shoes that are giving them blisters.

"Excited?" asks Zed, who's waiting patiently in the aisle as I move a chair away from the end of the row to make room for him.

"Not really," I say, but we grin at each other, both knowing that's a lie.

I am excited. Our mini-movie is a bit grainy and wobbly in places but it's fun. Everything went brilliantly with the filming on Wednesday. Swan and Zed planned our schedule perfectly and every last pupil, teacher, goat, dog and gran played their part. (Mademoiselle Fabienne was the hair and make-up artist, Toshio and Lulu managed the catering – i.e. took along a picnic of bananas, crisps and squash – and Twinkle and Downboy gamboled about very appealingly in the woods sections.)

Maybe other schools will have slick productions with fancy effects. Maybe they found super-impressive locations that we didn't know about. But we at St Grizzle's did the best we could and are proud of it.

And when I sent Arch the link to the finished film last night, he texted me THIS as soon as he'd watched it...

...and you can't get higher praise than that!

"Poo! Do you smell something, guys?" says a familiar voice. "Oh, it's just those loser Grizzlers. Ready to cheer when we win, you lot?"

Sigh

Spencer and his mates from the village school are hovering in the aisle.

They're acting all cocky because Lulu, Swan and the teachers are down at the other end of the row, trying to settle the over-excited Newts, which is a bit like expecting puppies to concentrate on learning times tables.

Totally ignoring Spencer and his cronies, I sit down with a small thump, while Zed's rubber wheels squeak on the polished floor as he manoeuvres into the space I made for him.

"So, where's your goat today, Grizzlers?" Spencer asks.

"So, where's your brain today, Spencer?" I mutter under my breath and Zed sniggers.

Twinkle and Downboy are in the coach, actually, which Granny Viv is parking now, after dropping us off. They were supposed to stay at school with Toshio but he got caught up in a game of Candy Crush and didn't notice Blossom and her buddies luring them out of the building with slices of cold pizza and sneaking them onboard the coach. They were so well hidden in the back row of seats that no one noticed there was a dog and a goat onboard till halfway to Dunchester Town Hall, when Downboy caught sight of a shih-tzu out of the back window and went barking bonkers, and Twinkle got excited and started galloping up and down the aisle. But I'm not wasting my time telling Spencer that.

"And what about the new Grizzler?" Spencer carries right on. "The old wrinkly one?"

"Yoo-hoo! I'm RIGHT here, darling!" Granny Viv booms at the top of her voice, striding down the aisle towards Spencer and his mates. "Did you miss me, sweetheart?"

EVERYONE in the hall turns to stare.

EVERY square inch of Spencer's face turns prawn pink.

I guess it's one thing to yell rude stuff at people from a distance but it's another when they're steamrolling right up to you and causing you maximum embarrassment.

"Hi! Hi, there!" Granny Viv continues to boom, waggling her fingers at the watching audience, who're clearly enjoying this pre-awards ceremony entertainment. "Can I have your attention for just a second?"

With her other hand, she swiftly grabs Spencer's arm, and – before he can protest or escape – holds it up in the air like he's a boxing champion or something.

"I just want to say good luck to *all* the schools here today," Granny Viv calls out, "but keep a special eye out for the film made by my friend here, Spender!"

"Spencer," mutters the prawn-pink boy.

"Spender's film... Well, there's a certain something about it that'll make it stand out. Trust me."

The audience stares at "Spender", who seems to be shrivelling before their very eyes, like a time-lapse clip of a prune. Then Granny Viv lets go of his arm and merrily shuffles along the row to the empty seat beside me.

"Well, that was..." I begin, without knowing how to describe it.

"Harsh but fair, dear," says Granny Viv. "Sweetie?"

"Er, thanks," I say, dipping my hand into the box of chocolates she's shoved under my nose. I'm about to ask what she meant by bigging up Spencer's film just now, when the lights go down and some suited women and men appear on the stage.

"Welcome to the Why We Love Where We Live film-screening and awards ceremony!" says one of the women.

Lots of whooping and applause breaks out, along with a wolf howl, which I suspect might be the work of a wolf cub called Blossom.

"Myself and the other judges from the council have SO enjoyed watching your films. You've all put such a lot of thought and effort into them. Now what we're going to do is let you all enjoy watching each other's work and then it'll be time to announce the winner!"

More cheers, more howling and a loud whoop!, whoop! from Swan, who's already decided we

should spend the prize money on a state-of-the-art movie screen and projector (plus deluxe popcorn maker) if we win.

And so it goes dark and silent, apart from the occasional wolf whimper as the teachers try and shush Blossom.

The first film starts up.

It is by a school from a village I don't know.

Various kids from the school walk around the delights of their village and show them off. These delights include a pretty church, a scenic old bridge, a war memorial and a duck pond on the green.

At the end we all hurrah and applaud, and then it's time for film two.

It is by another school, in another village we don't know.

Various kids from THIS school walk around the delights of THEIR village and show them off. These delights include a pretty church, a war memorial, a green with *no* duck pond this time and a market cross.

Films three to ten are roughly all the same, give or take a duck pond or rickety old bridge. (At the end of film seven, Zed whispered, "Didn't we see this one already?" because they're all so similar. I knew we hadn't, but only because the students in it wore striped yellow ties and we hadn't seen any of those in the previous films.)

"Thank you! Wonderful stuff!" says the woman from the council now, just like she's said after each of the films. "And now we're going to watch entry number eleven, by St Grizelda's School for Girls!"

"WHAAAAAAA!"

"YAYYYY!"

"HOW-WOOOOOO...!"

Our school – teeny as it is – makes the most noise of the ceremony so far, which is good really, since it pretty much drowns out the booing coming from across the aisle, from the direction of "Spender".

The woman who's hosting steps aside and our film begins, opening with the ghostly form of Miss Amethyst standing beside the statue of St Grizelda. I made sure St Grizzle was dressed appropriately for her film debut by scrubbing off the black crayon moustache someone had drawn on her.

A few murmured "Oooh!"s of interest ripple around the audience, which is pretty good going, considering I've been hearing a couple of quiet snores during the last few, more-or-less identical film entries.

"Hello," says Miss Amethyst, in her best dramatic posh voice. "I am the ghost of Miss Augusta Wilberbuttle, the first head teacher of St Grizelda's School for Girls."

More "Oohing!". Great!

"This fine school opened its doors in 1905. But over the years, when I've drifted back to haunt the place, I've noticed a lot of changes nearby…"

And now the scene switches.

We move to "Miss Wilberbuttle" talking in front of the ugly car park, with the triplets sitting on the wall behind her, doing their best eerie stares. There are a few other shots in front of several other concrete blocks, with smatterings of Newts in the background, kicking stones and acting generally bored. May-Belle's growly goth music grumbles moodily in the background.

Then we flip to the contrast scenes in the woods.

Soft guitar strumming accompanies the visuals (courtesy of Mademoiselle Fabienne).

Now "Miss Wilberbuttle" is pictured by the babbling waterfall, talking about its timeless beauty, then she's whisked off by the magic of editing to a tranquil wildlife pond, then to the truly magical fairy ring of mushrooms, after which she shows us the most touching carvings in the bark of trees, with lovelorn couples' names in hearts dating back to the 1800s.

We finish with a scene of "Miss Wilberbuttle" on top of a stony outcrop, her ghostly cape wafting in the breeze as she stares out over the treetops at the golden afternoon sun...

The credits roll, the camera pans down and in the clearing below we see children laughing and playing and – yes, even cartwheeling.

The lights go up and the room erupts into cheers and whoops.

I look at Zed and he's grinning so hard his face is in danger of splitting in two. I turn and gaze along our row and see matching manic grins beaming back at me. "Well done, Dani, darling," says Granny Viv, applauding madly. "You did a great job."

"Well, YOU came up with the idea," I remind her.

"Oh, the idea was only the first part," she says, shrugging off any credit. "YOU made the whole thing come together. I knew you would, Dani. You're just like your mum – a pair of shy girls, both of you, never realizing what you're capable of. I used to have to give your mum a nudge, too, sometimes, just to start her off if she was feeling unsure about things. I've always been happy to be the annoying loud person, if it gets you two going!"

I stare at Granny Viv ... so she DOES know just how "too much" she can sometimes be. It's funny to realize, too, that people can be annoying and brilliant and lots of other tricky and lovely things all at once, and that's OK...

"Thanks, Granny Viv!" I say, resting my head on her shoulder.

"You're quite welcome, my—"

"Shhhhhhh!" comes a hissed shush from Spencer's direction.

I look up. The woman who's hosting is now back onstage and is introducing the last film of the afternoon, which just happens to be Spencer's.

Up pops his smug, super-confident face on screen, right in front of the market cross. Urgh! I feel like closing my eyes till this is over…

"Ha!" Zed bursts out.

I look back at the screen – and immediately see what's so funny.

Spencer has been photobombed.

"The ancient stone cross has been here for centuries," Spencer drones on screen.

In the background, beyond the stone cross, a woman with red hair has just done a star jump.

Ripples of laughter echo across the hall.

They continue to ripple, getting louder, as the scene changes to Spencer in front of the bridge.

"It's said that a famous highwayman once used Huddleton Bridge as an escape route, galloping across it on his horse," says Spencer.

Behind him, that same red-haired woman crosses the bridge in the style of a kangaroo.

There are more scenes – Spencer by the duck pond, Spencer by the war memorial, Spencer by the old church – and every single time, Granny Viv is in the background, goofing around without him seeing her.

She must've done this yesterday, during that half hour she left me at the supermarket.

"This is **GENUIS!**" whispers Zed, though it's hard to hear him above the cheering and whoops.

"This is **TERRIBLE!**" I hear Spencer roar at his friends. "How could you let this happen?"

"I was just concentrating on you when I was filming!" I hear one of them protest.

"And you edited the film yourself," another chips in. "You wouldn't let any of us near it. So why didn't YOU notice, Spencer?"

The laughing and roaring is going crazy and it takes ages for the host lady to calm everyone down.

"Well," she says, when the huge room is finally, almost quiet. "We've certainly had an entertaining afternoon, haven't we? But now it's time to announce our winner, the short film that will feature on the council's new-look website. And that winner is..."

The whole of our row is vibrating and I peek down to see Swan's leg thud-a-dud-a-dudding in excitement. She can already imagine being slouched on a beanbag in the school hall, watching movies on our state-of-the-art-screen while eating piping-hot sugary popcorn, I can tell.

"...ST GRIZELDA'S SCHOOL FOR GIRLS!"

I don't even know how I make it up onstage. All I know is it's like being a rock star, carried and bundled through a crowd of fans.

But a few seconds later, I find myself surrounded by Newts, Conkers, Otters and Fungi – except for Zed, who's down below taking photos – and having a microphone shoved in my hand.

Erk

I think I'm meant to make a speech...

"Um," I start nervously – then I see Granny Viv give me the thumbs up and I find my voice (which is good, since this is my chance to properly thank my friends for getting behind me).

"I'd just like to say this film has been a ton of fun to do," I begin. "Well, it *was*, once we all pulled together. Cos a person on their own can do good things but when you work as a team, things can turn out pretty special."

I turn either side of me to wave at my schoolmates, who beam, yelp, jump or punch the air at my words.

"And apart from this lot," I yell into the mike, above their noise, "I'd like to thank St Grizzle's, ghosts and my runaway gran for making it all possible!"

My speech is short but it works and the applause is deafening.

I'm so bedazzled and bewildered that I barely register our prize as we all stumble off the stage and head back to our seats.

Chapter 12
"We Are the Champiioonnss..."

And a great big yeeehaaa...!

It might've been a good idea to pack earplugs for the coach on the way home.

The volume is DEAFENING.

At least Granny Viv managed to harness the extreme excitement of the Newts by switching on the coach's microphone and suggesting they sing a song instead of just screeching randomly and wolf howling.

And so everyone is now singing along at the top of their voices to *We Are the Champions*. I think this is the sixth time in a row. Downboy is joining in with a doggy yodel or two.

Actually, not everyone is joining in. The triplets are just swaying in their seats in time to the beat. Twinkle is *almost* chewing in time to the beat, as she sits on the floor up by Granny Viv, eating an Upcoming Events brochure that Miss Amethyst picked up at the Town Hall and thought she'd flick through on the journey back to school.

Swan isn't singing either. She's sulking. She had her heart set on turning our school hall into an in-house cinema and even though we won the competition, she'll still be watching the slightly fuzzy-screened old TV in the living room with the rest of us, since our prize turned out to be a trophy.

I'm not singing either. That's cos I'm huddled over in my seat, trying to talk to Arch.

"Show me this trophy, then!" he says, as he smiles up from my lap where my phone is perched. He's bouncing a bit as he talks – I've caught him as he's walking home from school.

"Ta-da!" I say, focusing in on it for him.

"Cool – looks big and shiny!" Arch shouts at me.

Oops, my best friend is not getting a true sense of proportion here. So I put the trophy alongside my head.

"Ahh…" he says with a slow nod of
understanding.

Because the trophy may be shiny but it is not
big.

If it didn't have a top, it would be perfect as
an egg cup.

"Did you have to make a speech?" asks Arch.

"Uh-huh," I say and feel myself blushing. I thought Zed was just taking photos at the ceremony but he'd actually filmed what I said. It's pretty embarrassing but I'm going to send it on to Mum later, so she can see what I've been up to...

"Dani?" I hear Lulu say.

"Gotta go – call you back later," I tell Arch, ending the call.

I smile at our head teacher, who has now crouched down to talk to me.

"Dani, can I ask your permission to do something?" she says.

"Huh? You want MY permission?" I repeat, confused. "Why?"

"Well, in the words of our founding head teacher, the fabulous Miss Wilberbuttle, a St Grizelda girl is valued. Your opinion is valuable, Dani, as is the opinion of every other girl—"

"—and *boy*, Mum," adds Zed, who is sitting next to me.

"Sorry, you're quite right, Zed," Lulu replies, happy to be corrected. "Everyone's opinions are valuable at our school and that's why I'd like your permission before I do something."

"All right," I say shyly but with a ripple of a thrill at being treated like an adult.

"I'd like to ask your grandmother if she'd consider staying on at St Grizzle's for the rest of this term while you're here, Dani. She's been SUCH a help the last couple of days and I don't just mean with the cooking and the housework. She has such a wonderful energy about her that I think will make her a perfect fit for us all at St—"

"YES!" I blurt out before Lulu can finish.

Granny Viv might be a bit of a loud, over-the-top, sometimes irritatingly huge character but she's MY loud, over-the-top, sometimes irritatingly huge character and I love her.

And if she gets too much, I'm grown-up and confident enough now to tell her.

Or I can ask Swan to.

"Lovely! I'll go and put it to her. Wish me luck!" says Lulu, pushing herself upright again and wobbling back down the aisle to the front of the coach.

I'm pretty sure what Granny Viv's answer will be.

I'm pretty sure she's been pretty lonely back home, with Mum and me gone and only Downboy to tell her jokes to.

Still, I lean out over Zed with my camera so I can film her reaction to what Lulu is saying.

Only I can't zoom in on it properly, because a wibbly-wobbly Mexican wave has started and all I can make out are girls' arms wafting wildly.

But that doesn't matter, because a moment

later a loud "**YEEEE–HAAAAAAAAAAAAA!**" bursts from the front of the coach.

Hmm, seems like me and Lulu have our answer.

And I'll be sending Mum yet another mini-film today, showing her that right this cowboy-whooping moment, Granny Viv is the newest recruit at St Grizzle's School for Girls, Ghosts, and Runaway Grannies...

Shhh...
How about a
sneak peek at the
next story in
the series?

I knew something was wrong with my best friend Arch when he posted zombies made out of loo-roll tubes on our YouTube channel.

He'd drawn goggle-eyed zombie faces on the cardboard tubes (he's a really good artist) and added wooden lolly-stick arms on them, but his living-dead monsters didn't really do much.

They just looked glum and grey as they inched towards the camera...

"What's this, Dani? Something new from Arch?" asks my classmate Swan, flopping down on the dorm bed beside me while I watch the film again and try to figure out why it's bothering me. "Hmm ... looks a bit gloomy, doesn't it? Not like his normal funny stuff."

Swan is **right**.

Since I got sent away to boarding school, me and Arch have kept in touch in all the usual ways, like messaging and texts and video chats. But most of all, we make and post dumb-but-fun mini-movies for each other to see.

The last one I posted was an action scene from James Bond. I made a tiny tuxedo out of black tissue paper for my little plastic Brontosaurus, then dangled it from Swan's twin brother's remote-controlled helicopter with a bit of leftover gift-wrap ribbon I found in the art room. While I filmed, Zed expertly worked the console and made my Secret Agent Dinosaur 007 swoop and zip around the back lawn of the school.

It was excellent, even **after** the helicopter crash-landed in a rhododendron bush and Swan had to rescue it before Twinkle the school goat leaped in and ate it. (Actually, that was the best bit.)

My James Bond epic was in reply to a mini-movie Arch had posted of himself having a conversation with a sock puppet. I only realized it was meant to be ME when I spotted the brown wool plaits he'd pinned to either side.

It was so cute, especially when another sock puppet – made to look like my fuzzly furred dog Downboy – **boinged** into the frame and chased sock-puppet Dani around the table. And it got even funnier when my old teacher, Miss Solomon, loomed into shot behind Arch saying, "Well, THIS doesn't look much like converting fractions to decimals to ME, Archie Kaminski!" before yanking both the socks off his hands in one swift move.

"Y'know, I **definitely** think something's up with Arch," I mumble, pressing my cursor and watching the teeny-weeny zombies lurch moodily towards me again.

"Still not talked to him in a while?" asks Swan.

"Nope. It's been two whole days now," I reply, as Swan lazily blows and **POPs!** one of her perfect pink bubbles of gum. "I guess I'll have to try the last resort..."

"Which is?" asks Swan, twirling elasticy strings of gum around her finger.

"Calling him on his home phone later," I tell her, dreading it already.

What if one of Arch's parents pick up? They have been SO weird since I left, a whole not-quite-a-month ago.

Mr Kaminski – Arch's normally joke-a-minute dad – sounds all sad and forlorn whenever he answers the phone to me now, like I am a condemned prisoner who's been given a life sentence, instead of a ten-year-old girl who's having to spend a term at St Grizelda's School for Girls while her mum's on an expedition to the Antarctic.

Mrs Kaminski is even worse... I swear she sounds all choked and teary when she talks to me.

She really doesn't approve of Mum sending her beloved only child away to boarding school.

To be honest, when I first heard Mum's plan to send me here, I didn't approve of it either. But even though I've tried to explain what it's actually like here, Mrs Kaminski doesn't seem to believe that St Grizzle's isn't a strict 'n' stern, no-fun, no-magictastic version of Hogwarts.

I mean, if only she could see the posh, stone statue of St Grizelda out in the driveway at the front of the school ... this morning she has an orange Christmas cracker paper hat taped to her head and a plastic shopping bag dangling from each of her outstretched hands.

If only Mrs Kaminski could meet Lulu the head teacher, whose uniform today is a faded "Hello Kitty" T-shirt, frayed-edge denim shorts and flip-flops with giant plastic daisies on them.

If only she could see the goblin flying past the

dorm window on a trapeze right now, screaming its head off (in other words, eight-year-old Blossom from Newts Class getting ready for our whole-school lesson in circus skills).

But of course Mr and Mrs Kaminski's opinions of my new school don't matter as much as discovering what's going on with my friend Arch.

Just why do I get the feeling he's as gloomy as his loo-roll zombies?

Like James (Brontosaurus) Bond, it's my mission to find out...

Dani's in for a surprise when Arch turns up at St Grizzle's acting weird and unhappy. How can Dani make him feel like he fits in at the school and not to be put out by her new friendships? It sems like her old life and her new life are colliding and not in a GOOD WAY. With all her favourite people in one place (almost) life should be fantastic, shouldn't it...?

St Grizzle's School for Girls, Geeks and Tag-along Zombies
— coming soon!

STUDENTS

FUNGI CLASS

STUDENTS

CONKERS CLASS

Yas

Angel

Klara

May-Belle

OTTERS CLASS

The Triplets

STUDENTS

NEWTS CLASS

SCHOOL PETS

Twinkle

Downboy

Karen McCombie

Karen McCombie is the best-selling author of a gazillion* books for children, tweens and teens, including series such as the much-loved 'Ally's World' and gently bonkers 'You, Me and Thing', plus novels *The Girl Who Wasn't There* and *The Whispers of Wilderwood Hall.*

Born in Scotland, Karen now lives in north London with her very Scottish husband Tom, sunshiney daughter Milly and beautiful but bitey cat Dizzy.

Karen loves her job, but is a complete fidget. She regularly packs up her laptop and leaves Office No. 1 (her weeny back bedroom) and has a brisk walk to Office No. 2 (the local garden centre café).

Her hobbies are stroking random cats in the street, smiling at dogs and eating crisps.

You can find her waffling about books, cats and bits & bobs at…

www.karenmccombie.com
Facebook: KarenMcCombieAuthor
Instagram: @karenmccombie
Twitter: @KarenMcCombie

*Okay, more than 80, if you're going to get technical.

Author
Factfile

- **Favourite thing about being an author:**
  Ooh, doing school visits, where I can meet lovely real people, instead of staring at wordies on a computer all day.

- **Second most favourite thing about being an author:**
  Eating cake while I'm writing at Office No. 2 (i.e. my local garden centre café).

- **Best question ever asked during an event:**
  "What's your favourite flavour of crisps?"
  (My answer was ALL crisps are good crisps, but ready salted will always win my heart...)

- **Tell us a secret!**
  Early on at school, I was rubbish at reading and writing because of an undiagnosed hearing problem. From the age of five to six, I basically sat in class wondering what on earth was going on around me. It took an operation and a lot of catching up before I learned to read and write well.

- **Favourite waste of time:**
  Dancing whenever I get the chance, much to my daughter's shame (like THAT'S going to stop me!).

Becka
Moor

Becka Moor is an illustrator/author from Manchester, where they say things like 'innit' and 'that's mint, that' when something is really good. She managed to escape the North for a couple of years and ended up in Wales (which, as it happened, was still up North) where she studied Illustration for Children's Publishing at Glyndwr University. Since moving back home, Becka has set up shop in a little home office where she works on all kinds of children's books, including the 'Violet and the Pearl of the Orient' series and *The Three Ninja Pigs* picture book. When she's not hunched over a drawing or pondering which texture to apply to a dragon poo, she can be found chasing her two cats around the house begging for cuddles, or generally making a mess.

You can find more useless information in these dark corners of the interwebs:

www.beckamoor.com
Twitter: @BeckaMoor
Blog: www.becka-moor.tumblr.com

Illustrator Factfile

- **Favourite thing about being an illustrator:**
  Drawing all day!
- **Second most favourite thing about being an illustrator:**
  Getting to read lots of brilliant stories and imagining
  how the characters might look.
- **Tell us something odd!**
  I have a mug collection so huge that the whole world
  could come to my house for tea at the same time, but
  someone else would have to provide the biscuits!
  I'll have a Hobnob or five, please.
- **Favourite waste of time:**
  Baking. It's only a waste of time because I can't bake and
  whatever comes out of the oven is usually inedible!

Find out how Dani first ends
up at St Grizzle's in...

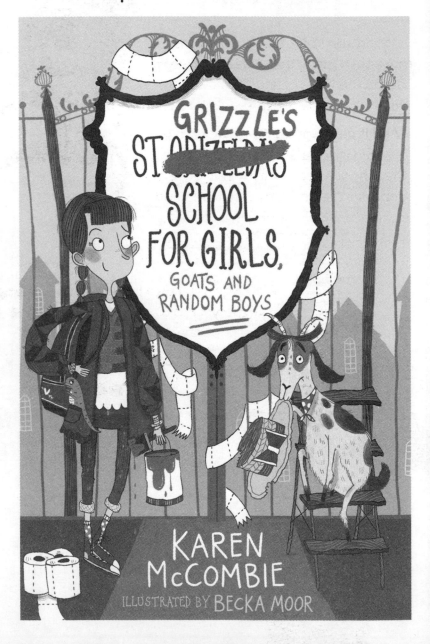

GRIZZLE'S

ST ~~GRIZELDA'S~~

SCHOOL
FOR GIRLS,
GOATS AND
RANDOM BOYS

KAREN
McCOMBIE

ILLUSTRATED BY BECKA MOOR

My mum loves penguins' bums more than me. Otherwise she'd never dump me in some stuffy old school while she heads off to the Antarctic.

And it gets worse. When we arrive at St Grizelda's School for Girls, the school's had a drastic makeover. Gone are the uniforms, the rules and ... er, most of the pupils and staff. In their place is TOTAL CHAOS.

We're greeted by a bunch of stampeding eight-year-olds, a head-butting goat and a crazy head teacher wearing a plastic-spoon crown.

Somebody get me OUT of here!